DEADLY CONFRONTATION

Lassie moved into the thicket and edged between two bushes to a point where she had a clear view of the area. Then she saw it—a full-grown male cougar, a ferocious-looking beast with several hundred pounds of rippling muscles and razor-sharp fangs.

The cougar gave a low snarl and came forward slowly, every muscle tensed, its eyes vertical slits of flashing red. Lassie knew her only chance was to bluff her way through; to show no fear. She had picked the spot— the soft white fur between the cougar's chin and shoulders. With her heart pounding and the adrenalin surging through her body, she braced herself, her teeth bared, ready to duck below the opened claws and flashing fangs . . .

THE MAGIC OF LASSIE

Lassie comes back . . .
in an exciting new fun-filled film

Jack Wrather
Presents

THE MAGIC OF LASSIE

Mickey Rooney   Pernell Roberts

Stephanie Zimbalist   Michael Sharrett

Alice Faye   Gene Evans

The Mike Curb
Congregation   and of course,
Lassie

James Stewart as Clovis Mitchell

Music and Lyrics by Richard M. Sherman
and Robert B. Sherman

Music Supervised, Arranged
and Conducted by Irwin Kostal

Story by Robert B. Sherman
& Richard M. Sherman

Screenplay by Jean Holloway,
Robert B. Sherman & Richard M. Sherman

Produced by Bonita Granville Wrather
and William Beaudine, Jr.

Directed by Don Chaffey

Dolby Stereo

Color by CFI

Released by The International Picture Show Company

THE MAGIC OF LASSIE

A NOVEL BY ROBERT WEVERKA

Based on the screenplay by
**JEAN HOLLOWAY, ROBERT B. SHERMAN
and RICHARD M. SHERMAN**

From a story by
**ROBERT B. SHERMAN
& RICHARD M. SHERMAN**

BANTAM BOOKS
TORONTO · NEW YORK · LONDON

THE MAGIC OF LASSIE
A Bantam Book / December 1978
2nd printing
3rd printing

ISBN 0-553-12617-2

Published simultaneously in the United States and Canada

Bantam Book are published by Bantam Books, Inc. Its trade-
mark, consisting of the words "Bantam Books" and the por-
trayal of a bantam, is registered in the United States Patent
Office and in other countries. Marca Registrada. Bantam
Books, Inc., 666 Fifth Avenue, New York, New York 10019.

THE MAGIC OF LASSIE

1

Without lifting her head, Lassie opened her eyes for a minute and gazed sleepily across the dark bedroom. The sky outside was growing pale and a faint reddish tint bathed the branches of the poplar tree by the window.

In the bed, ten-year-old Chris Mitchell was still asleep, his arm stretched out and his fingers buried in the thick fur of Lassie's neck.

She didn't move. Her chin was resting on the floor between her front paws, and with her eyes only half open she listened to the chirps and flutterings of the wakening birds outside.

The house was still silent. Usually she could hear the soft drone of Grandpa's snoring in the next bedroom, or by this time Kelly would be up and getting dressed in the room across the hall. But everyone seemed to be enjoying an extra ten minutes of sleep this morning. With a long sigh Lassie closed her eyes and dozed with them. Then her ears suddenly snapped erect and she lifted her head, listening.

From somewhere downstairs, in the kitchen, there had been a faint creaking of the floor. Then she heard the soft click of the back door being closed.

She moved carefully, edging out from under Chris' hand, and crossed to the door. With a front paw braced on the wall, she gripped the knob in her teeth, turned it slightly and pulled. The door opened a crack and she nosed her way through.

She knew it was Grandpa who had gone out the back door. It was a game they played; Grandpa getting dressed as quietly as he could and trying to sneak out of the house without Lassie hearing him. More often than not Lassie heard the first creaking of bedsprings and she was waiting and wagging her tail in the hallway when he came through his bedroom door. But this morning he had fooled her; she knew he was already striding through the vineyards to the top of the hill behind the house.

Without a moment's hesitation, Lassie bounded down the stairs and into the entry hall. After she maneuvered the front door open and pushed through the screen door, she loped around the corner of the house and took off at full speed through the vineyards.

Grandpa laughed when he saw her coming. He was standing at the top of the hill, grinning, his old felt hat pushed to the back of his head. "Well, well, well . . . look at the old sleepyhead. Where you been, Lassie?"

Clovis Mitchell was tall and lean, his face as creased and weathered as one of Chris' old baseball mitts. He was wearing his patched gray sweater this morning, and he knelt and gave Lassie's head and neck a good welcoming scratch when she reached his side. Her whole body wriggled and twisted as she wagged her tail and panted and rubbed against his leg.

"How you feeling this morning, girl?"

Lassie barked and circled around him once more, letting him know she felt fine. With a look of satisfaction Clovis straightened and gazed out at the fields and the hills beyond.

For sixty-two years Clovis Mitchell had lived in California's Sonoma Valley and, just as his father and grandfather had done before him, he rose at dawn every morning and climbed the highest hill in the vineyards.

No doubt the grapes would have grown as fat and sweet and juicy and produced the same fine wines without his daily inspection. But Clovis had a strong feeling of kinship with the vines. Over the years he had nursed them through flood and drought and disease and the plague of insects, and they were almost as much a part of the family as Chris and Kelly and Lassie. Now, with the sun just beginning to show itself on the eastern horizon, the rolling, vine-covered hills sparkled like a deep, golden-green carpet.

Barring any kind of unforeseen disaster, it was going to be a bumper crop this year. The grapes were rich and full, hanging in massive bunches from the vines, and within a day or two—or maybe three—they would be ready for harvesting.

At the moment it was the sky to the northwest that occupied Clovis' attention. The clouds were beautiful to look at; a billowing mass rising like heaps of whipped cream above the horizon. But the thick layer of gray on the underside had an ominous look. In these last critical days while the grapes were ripening, they needed plenty of sunshine, and any prolonged rain could be disastrous.

Clovis studied the configuration for several minutes, trying to determine if the clouds were moving, and if so in what direction. At his side, Lassie, following the direction of his gaze, was peering intently at the sky.

"What do you think?" Clovis asked.

Lassie gave him a questioning glance as if she wasn't too certain. A sudden bang of the screen door drew their attention to the house.

Clovis smiled as he saw Chris come striding up the slope. The boy's hair was still mussed from sleep, and he was stuffing his T-shirt into his jeans. Except when they went to church on Sundays, Clovis couldn't remember Chris wearing anything but jeans and tennis shoes during the summer. Chris was a little small for his age, but it didn't seem to bother him. Very likely he would start growing an inch a week one of these days, and end up taller than his father had been.

Clovis sometimes marveled at the strength and resiliency of Chris and his sister, Kelly. Four years ago, when Chris was six and Kelly only fifteen, their mother and father had been killed in an automobile accident. It was one of those freak things that was nobody's fault. They were driving home from Santa Rosa in a heavy rainstorm and a bridge had washed out only minutes before they came to it. It was the most tragic and difficult time in all of their lives, and every day Clovis gave thanks for the strength God had given him and his grandchildren, and for the kindness and generosity of the neighbors and townspeople of Glen Ellen.

There was a frown on Chris' freckled face this morning. He was glancing off at the same clouds Lassie and Clovis had been studying.

"Mornin', Grandpa, mornin', Lassie. What do you think of those clouds over yonder, Grandpa?"

"I'm not sure," Clovis answered. "What do you think?"

"I think we'd better keep our eyes on 'em."

Clovis nodded. "Yep, rain could be fatal at this stage of the game." With Chris and Lassie following him, he moved a few paces down the hill and studied a heavy cluster of grapes.

"They ready for harvest?" Chris asked.

Clovis picked a grape and bit into it, letting the juices linger on his tongue. The sugar content of the grapes was the most important factor in making good wine. Clovis popped the rest of the grapes in his mouth and shook his head. "Not yet," he said.

"How soon do you think, Grandpa?"

"Maybe three days—give or take a day."

Lassie was glancing from one to the other as if carefully considering the situation. Then she looked sharply toward the house and lifted her nose. Smelling something particularly good, she gave a happy bark and headed down the slope at full speed. An instant later Kelly came out the back door and banged on a steel triangle. "Bacon and eggs!" she shouted.

Clovis laughed as they started down. "You have to have a lot of respect for that dog's nose."

Lassie bolted through the door as quickly as Kelly headed back in. She knew Kelly would have filled her bowl already, and breakfast was her favorite meal. On the polished linoleum she skidded a few feet to make the corner, and then she dug in with no formalities. Along with the canned dogfood there were crumbled biscuits covered with gravy and a few chunks of meat from last night's supper. As the others came in, Lassie paused long enough to give them a panting smile, then dug in again.

"Dear Lord," Clovis said a few minutes later, "we thank Thee for what we are about to receive and, if it isn't asking too much, please don't let it rain. And don't let the winds blow, and keep the temperature steady until after harvest. Amen."

"And please keep the bugs and birds away," Chris added.

"Amen to that, too," Clovis said. "You have anything to add, Kelly?"

Kelly smiled and unfolded her napkin. "No, Grandpa, I think you and Chris covered it all."

Lassie had lowered her own head a little but she

watched closely, waiting for grace to be finished. Then she moved over to a spot between Grandpa and Chris.

Chris gave her a quick pat on the head. "What's the matter, Lassie? Kelly starving you this morning?"

Lassie yelped anxiously, then crossed to the corner and brought back her empty bowl.

Clovis laughed. "Yep. It's empty, all right. I guess Kelly forgot to feed you." Both he and Chris dropped a half piece of bacon into it.

"You know what you're all getting, don't you?" Kelly said as she also made a contribution. "One great big snow job."

Lassie dropped the bowl to the floor and quickly devoured the bacon before anybody changed his mind. Then she stretched out and rested her head between her paws. She knew that was all the begging she could get away with, but she continued watching, just in case.

"It's going to be a great crop," Clovis said while he spread jam over his toast. "My nose tells me. And my fingers. This is finally going to be the great one!"

Kelly smiled. "You say that every year, Grandpa."

"Well, this is the year I'm gonna be right."

"That's what you told us last year." Chris laughed.

Clovis smiled, knowing it was true. But deep in his heart he had a strong feeling about it this year. He had never seen the grapes quite so plump and heavy and with such good color. If the weather held, he had no doubts about being right. "You'll see," he said confidently.

"After I get the house cleaned up I'm going into town today," Kelly said. "You two want to come along?"

"You got some legal business you have to take care of?" Clovis asked.

Kelly's face reddened a little and she busied herself cleaning up her plate. "Oh, Grandpa! Of course not."

The last three or four times they had gone to town Clovis had noticed that Kelly always found some excuse to walk by the office of a young lawyer named Allan Fogerty. And Allan Fogerty always found time to hurry out and say hello.

Clovis guessed he might be a little prejudiced in the matter, but in his opinion Kelly was the prettiest girl inside five hundred miles of Glen Ellen. She also had a lot of good sense. As far as Allan Fogerty was concerned, the young man seemed bright and ambitious, and Clovis had an idea there might be some hand-holding and serious courting before long.

"Well," he said, "I wouldn't mind going along. There's a few things I'd like to pick up before harvesting starts."

"I'd like to go too," Chris said. He glanced at Clovis and quickly added. "As soon as I get the garden weeded."

Lassie came to her feet and gave a short excited bark. She was always ready for a ride, and she particularly liked to see what was going on in town.

After breakfast, Clovis went off to his laboratory to do some work with his foreman, Will Bradley, and Lassie followed Chris to the vegetable garden. It was a beautiful sunny day, and the clouds to the northwest didn't look like they had moved an inch.

While Chris pulled the weeds, Lassie moved a basket along to collect them. When the job was done, Chris got out a garden hose to water, and

Lassie moved a good distance away, not too fond of playing in the mud. She finally trotted over to Grandpa's laboratory and stretched out on the doormat. With the sun beating warmly on her heavy coat, she closed her eyes and sighed contentedly. Suddenly her nose crinkled, and she started to sniff curiously. She could smell the chemicals from inside Grandpa's laboratory. She could also smell the ripening grapes, and the last lingering scent of the breakfast Kelly had cooked. But there was something else in the air.

She lifted her head and looked out across the vineyard, her ears cocked for any strange sounds. There seemed to be nothing unusual. She held her head still for a minute, trying to catch the smell again, but it seemed to be gone now.

She finally rose and walked to the vineyard where she sat down and sniffed some more. She glanced around in all directions, but there still seemed to be nothing unusual. Pausing occasionally to sniff the air, she trotted along the edge of the field, moving toward the lower end of the vineyards. When she reached the dirt road bordering the property, she turned and followed it for another quarter of a mile. Then she stopped and held herself perfectly still. She smelled it again; a human scent, along with the lingering smell of a strange car. It seemed to be coming from the clump of trees a hundred yards ahead.

She trotted on, finally stopping when she reached the trees. The scent was strong now, and the imprint of fresh tire tracks showed clearly at the side of the road. She sniffed the dirt, then moved among the trees where she suddenly caught the strong scent of humans. Then she saw them; two sets of footprints leading into the vineyard. With her nose close to the ground, she followed them between a row of grapevines where they suddenly stopped. Lassie sniffed the dirt and the vines, and then saw the broken stem where a large cluster of grapes had been picked.

It was strange. Kids sometimes picked grapes from the vineyard when they were passing by, and Grandpa always said they were welcome to them. But these tracks had the smell of adults, and it seemed clear they had come and gone in a car. And for some reason the scent was vaguely familiar to Lassie.

She sniffed some more, following the tracks back to the trees—certain now that the scent was familiar. But it was from a long time ago; too long for her to place exactly. Except she had an uneasy feeling about it, as if she had once had an unpleasant experience with the person.

She sniffed at the tire tracks and moved further along the road, but then stopped as the tracks suddenly ended. Apparently the car had gone only as far as the trees; then, after the man picked the grapes, the car had been turned around and driven away. Lassie was still trying to pick up a trail when her ears perked up at the distant sound of Chris' voice.

"Lassie!" he shouted, "Come on, Lassie, we're leaving."

She took one last glance at the trees and broke into a run.

Kelly was just coming out the door with her purse when Lassie reached the house.

"Wash your hands and put on a clean shirt if you're coming with me," she said to Chris.

He was coiling the garden hose. "I already washed my hands," he said. "I washed them with the hose."

Kelly smiled. "Well wash them again with some soap. And don't forget to put the hoe away."

"All right, Kelly," Grandpa said with a laugh as he came out of the laboratory, "I'll wash my hands and put on a clean shirt."

"I didn't mean you, Grandpa."

"That's all right, honey. I know you want us to look our best when we go to town. In case we meet somebody important." He laughed and was inside the door before she could answer.

Once they were headed for town, Lassie forgot about the strange visitors. Sitting in back of the jeep, with the wind buffeting her face and whistling past her ears, was her favorite part of going for a ride. As they passed by the other farms, the men working in the vineyards waved, kids shouted at Chris and Lassie, and women hanging out clothes smiled from their backyards. Lassie barked while Kelly and Chris waved back, and Grandpa grinned and swerved around potholes and broke into song now and then.

Grandpa's singing voice wasn't much to listen to, and he talked the words as much as he sang them. But over the years of driving to town he had made up a song, and it seemed like the trip was never the same unless he sang it.

To get started he always took an extra deep breath of fresh air, then smiled and shook his head. "Oh, golly gee," he'd say, "I love that hometown feeling."

Then, while he swerved the jeep back and forth, he would grin and his voice would rise a little as he sang. The song was about never having to lock your door, and hearing the news at the grocery store, listening to the band play in the park, and all the other nice things about living in a small town.

Sometimes Chris and Kelly would join in, and by the time they reached the main road Lassie would yelp and howl along with them.

"I'll tell you what the whole world needs . . ." he would finish up, his voice almost at a shout. "More nickel cigars. Oh, yes—no faster speeds. This whole world needs that hometown feeling again--nn-n-n-n."

At the edge of town a little white church stood back off the road, surrounded by petunias, and they all waved as Father Ricardo smiled at them from the door. Then they passed over a stone bridge and, with Lassie barking urgently, Clovis pulled over to the side.

The bridge was only a few blocks from the middle of town, and Lassie always insisted on going the rest of the way on foot. She jumped down and loped away, and the rest of them drove on.

Her first stop was at a house a hundred yards farther along the road. An old man was digging in his garden; a gray poodle stretched out on the grass beside him. The poodle came instantly to his feet when he saw Lassie coming, but then he wagged his tail and eased back down. Both the dog and the man were so old, Lassie always liked to check in to see how they were doing.

They seemed to be getting along fine. The man looked up and grinned when he saw Lassie, and the dog gave her a panting smile. After a couple minutes of scratching and nudging, Lassie barked and moved on.

The next house was a little white bungalow that belonged to an elderly widow named Mrs. Kern. Lassie trotted up to the porch where she was knitting in her rocker and put her chin in the woman's lap.

The woman smiled and scratched Lassie's head. "Well, well, how nice to see you, Lassie. How are you feeling today?"

Lassie barked and wagged her tail, and Mrs. Kern laughed.

"If you ever get tired of those folks, you come live with me. All right?"

Lassie nudged her nose against the woman's hand and moved off.

She saw five or six more dogs and several more people before she finally reached the center of town. None of the family was in sight, but the jeep was parked by the post office. Lassie sat down and looked things over, panting contentedly.

The town of Glen Ellen was only three or four blocks long. In addition to the post office, there was a market and a general store and five or six other shops. Farther down, an ancient-looking building housed the sheriff and mayor's office, along with those of several private professional people. Lassie gazed at the building for a minute, and then, after a glance at Shone's Merchandise Store, where Kelly was probably shopping, she trotted down the street.

The office at the corner of the building had a small window with gilt lettering that said, ALLAN FOGERTY—ATTORNEY AT LAW. Lassie moved around to the side door and barked.

Allan Fogerty came out almost immediately. He was a big man with sandy hair, and looked more like a farmer than an attorney. But he had a broad, friendly smile, and his blue eyes sparkled with enthusiasm. He gave Lassie a hug as she jumped up and licked his face. "Hello, Lassie! Where's the rest of the family?"

Lassie barked and moved a few paces toward the street, then hesitated.

Allan smiled. "You want me to go with you?"

Lassie barked again, wagged her tail and moved a few more paces.

"Okay, girl, I'm coming."

Lassie trotted forward, head high, checking behind her now and then to make sure Allan was following. When she reached the door of Shone's store it suddenly opened, almost knocking her down. Kelly pushed her way out, both arms clutching heavy bags. Her face brightened as she saw Allan Fogerty.

"Why, Allan! What a surprise!"

Allan grinned and hurried forward to help. "Here, let me take those."

"We thought you were working on a case in Sonoma," Kelly said. "Imagine bumping into you like this!"

Allan smiled at Lassie. "Well, it isn't exactly by accident."

"Oh?"

"No. Lassie came and got me."

An orange toppled out as Allan took one of the bags. Like a shot, Lassie was after it and came back with her tail wagging.

"Where's your car?" Allan asked as he put the orange back.

"Over there by the post office."

Clovis was standing by the jeep now, his arm resting on the windshield. He reached over and gave the horn an impatient honk.

"Be right there, Grandpa," Kelly called out. But she didn't appear to be in a hurry as she and Allan crossed the street.

Allan asked how the grape crop was ripening.

"Good, I guess. Grandpa thinks it will be the best we ever had."

"That's good."

"Yes, he's very excited about it."

"Well, I hope it turns out as good as he expects."

Lassie trotted alongside, giving them an occasional glance when their conversation seemed to lag.

"It's a beautiful day, isn't it?" Kelly said.

"It sure is. But those dark clouds are still hanging around over there."

"Yes, Grandpa was a little worried about them this morning."

They had reached the jeep now and Clovis was squinting hard at them. "Say, I don't want to interrupt anything important, but we've been away from the grapes too long."

"Yes, sir," Allan said and put the bags in the back. "We were just talking about those clouds over there, Mr. Mitchell."

"That so?" Clovis said. He hit the horn again and Chris came flying across the street with a bag in his hand. He climbed into the back of the jeep and Lassie jumped in after him.

"Allan," Clovis said with a wry smile, "why don't you come out to supper and finish this conversation I'm interrupting? I'd be interested in hearing your opinion about those clouds."

"I'd like to do that, sir."

Kelly blushed and moved around to the passenger side.

"Come on about six," Clovis said.

"Yes, sir. Thank you."

"That all right with you, Kelly?" Clovis asked as he slid behind the wheel.

"That's fine, Grandpa." She kept her eyes straight ahead, but once Clovis backed out she gave Allan a quick smile and waved.

"Thanks, Lassie," Allan called out as they drove away.

2

"We've got some nice steaks in the freezer," Clovis said when they got home and carried the groceries into the kitchen. "Never met a man who didn't like a good thick steak."

"Oh, anybody can cook a steak, Grandpa. I was thinking about something like chicken cacciatore."

"What if he doesn't like chicken? And how come you never cooked that chicken catch- . . . catcha-whatever for us?"

"It just never occurred to me. And Allan went to college and everything. He probably has very sophisticated tastes."

Clovis laughed and went out the back door, leaving Kelly leafing through her cookbooks. From the way the two of them were looking at each other in town, he had an idea Kelly could cook a pot of hotdogs and Allan would think it was the greatest gourmet treat in the world.

Clovis headed for the hill again, and Lassie jumped up from where she was dozing and trotted along.

Clovis wanted to be dead-certain about the grapes. The clouds to the northwest had moved away without coming too close, and it had been an unusually warm morning. And with grapes you never knew. Sometimes within a matter of hours they would suddenly reach maturity. With a crop

15

this full and heavy, Clovis didn't want to take any chances.

Halfway up the slope he eased himself to one knee and studied a thick cluster for a minute. He touched a grape and pulled gently, snapping it from the stem. When he put it in his mouth and bit, his heart suddenly jumped. The juice was like pure sugar.

Lassie gazed questioningly at him, and Clovis snapped off another grape and let her have it. She gulped it down instantly and yelped for another.

Clovis laughed. "You'll never make a grape tester that way, Lassie." He gave her another, then tasted a second and a third, taking them from different vines. Then he grinned. "By golly, girl, they're perfect!" His heart pounding, he rose and headed down the slope, picking two or three more and tasting them. He was satisfied—they were all perfect. He was running now; Lassie galloping alongside and barking happily.

"Will!" Clovis shouted when he reached the winery. He pulled open the door and stuck his head in. "Will! We need pickers the first thing in the morning! The grapes are ready to burst their skins. Get on the phone—fast!"

Kelly and Chris were staring at him from the porch when he turned back. "Take it easy, Grandpa," Kelly said, "Your blood pressure will be going through the roof."

"You're darned right it will, Kelly! The grapes are ready and it's going to be the best crop anybody's ever seen in California!"

Kelly smiled, but she looked uneasy. "Maybe I'd better call Allan and tell him not to come tonight."

"Why?" Chris asked, "We aren't picking tonight."

"You bet we aren't." Clovis laughed. "Tonight we're celebrating!"

Caught up in the enthusiasm, Lassie trotted in circles and barked at all of them.

"Look at that," Clovis said. "Lassie knows too. It's our vintage year, isn't it, girl?" He grabbed Lassie's head and wrestled playfully with her for a minute. "Come on, Chris," he finally said, "we've got work to do."

Harvesting the grapes was always the most frantic time in the vineyards. When the pickers came they worked fast; a ton of grapes would be picked from every acre, and they had to be pressed quickly, and the juice pumped into settling tanks. From the tanks the juice was then decanted into hundreds of oak barrels to begin its first period of aging. The operation involved a great deal of hard work, and at each stage the juice had to be constantly checked to make certain there were no contaminants or unsuitable grapes.

To prepare for the hectic days ahead, Clovis and Chris and Will Bradley spent the rest of the afternoon giving a final cleaning to the presses and tanks, and making sure all the operating equipment was ready to go.

When Clovis started the tractor and pulled the big empty wagons out into the vineyard, Lassie jumped up and rode along. But when they started cleaning up the winery, Clovis made her stay outside. He didn't think people would appreciate dog hairs in their wine.

Lassie didn't mind. She went to the kitchen and had a bite to eat and then watched Kelly work on her dinner for awhile. Finally she wandered back outside and dozed in the sun. She opened her eyes occasionally and kept watch on the clump of trees down by the dirt road. But there were no cars parked there, and nobody passed by.

Once again she tried to remember the scent she had detected in the vineyard. It was a man; she

was sure of that. But it was from so long ago—
back when she was no more than a puppy—that
she just couldn't place it.

She finally rose and stretched herself, then
moved down to the edge of the fields and trotted
on to the road. When she reached the clump of
trees she caught the scent again, but it was not as
strong as it had been earlier in the day. Apparently
the man had not come back while they were in
town. She smelled more closely this time, moving
from the trees into the rows of grapevines, sniffing
once more at the broken stem where the man had
picked a clump of grapes. The identity of the
man still didn't come back to her. But the feeling
of dislike was now mixed with a little fear. For
someone to make what seemed like a special trip
to their vineyards just to pick a clump of grapes
was odd enough. But for that person to be someone from the distant and almost forgotten past
was even more strange.

Lassie lingered close to the trees for almost an
hour before Allan Fogerty's car appeared under a
distant cloud of dust. As soon as she recognized it,
Lassie loped toward the corner of the vineyard
where Allan would turn and head up to the house.

Allan smiled and came to a stop when he saw
her. "Hey, Lassie, what're you doing down here?
Want a lift?" He opened the door and she jumped
in, giving his face a lick.

"Hey, I just had a bath twenty minutes ago. I
don't need another one."

Lassie yelped and perched herself on the seat as
they drove on up to the house. Whatever Allan had
on his face smelled good, but it had a stinging, bitter taste when Lassie gave his cheek a quiet lick.
It was the same kind of stuff Clovis slapped on his
cheeks after he shaved and was getting dressed up
to go somewhere.

When the car stopped Lassie bounded up the

steps and opened the front door, but Allan rang the bell anyway. Lassie barked, letting him know it was all right to go in, but Allan still hung back until Kelly came to greet him. Lassie knew that Kelly and Allan were friends, but it would not have been apparent to an outsider.

Once they were seated in the living room, they spoke to each other like two strangers meeting for the first time. Kelly said she was very pleased that he could come to dinner, and Allan talked about what a nice house they had. Then Kelly told a deliberate lie that made Lassie's ears perk up.

"We're not having anything special tonight," she said, "I hope you don't mind. I just happened to have some chicken in the refrigerator and I made a little sauce to put on it."

"Chicken is one of my favorite dishes," he said. Then he jumped quickly to his feet as Clovis and Chris came down the stairs.

Clovis had shaved and put sweet-smelling stuff on his face, and Chris had dressed in different pants, and a regular shirt. After they sat down, Clovis told Allan all about the grapes being ready for harvest, and how this was going to be the best crop he ever had. Allan seemed happy about it, then they all went in the dining room to eat.

Lassie knew better than to beg in the dining room. She moved in quietly and settled herself near the wall, resting her chin on the floor, pretending to be indifferent to the food. But she watched closely as Kelly brought the bowls of vegetables and the steaming platter of chicken from the kitchen. Then Lassie lifted her head as Grandpa said something that turned Kelly's face red.

"You're a lucky man, Allan," he chuckled when Kelly finally sat down. "Kelly's been in that kitchen all afternoon making up some kind of special chicken for you. Chicken catcha-morry? Is that what you called it, Kelly?"

"It's chicken cacciatore, Grandpa, and it's nothing special at all. It's just chicken with Italian sauce on it, that's all."

"Well, it certainly looks good," Allan said.

Grandpa gave thanks for the food and the wonderful crop they were about to harvest. When he finished everybody dug in, and Lassie sighed and returned her chin to the floor.

When Kelly finally brought out pie and coffee, Lassie came quietly to her feet and edged to a position between Kelly and Allan. But nobody seemed to notice her.

Chris was the first to finish his dessert. He downed his milk and pushed his chair back. "Can Lassie and I be excused?"

Grandpa smiled. "Chris, suppose you and I do the dishes tonight. Wouldn't that be fun?"

"Fun?" Chris stared at Grandpa as if he had never heard such a crazy thing in his life. "Aw, Grandpa."

"There's fifty cents in it for you," Grandpa said and chuckled. "In my day it was a nickel, but I guess inflation has set in."

Kelly gave him a surprised look. "I don't want you to do the dishes."

"Well, that's too bad, young lady, because I'm gonna do 'em. Now you just run along. And you don't want to gyp Chris out of his fifty cents, do you?"

"I can use it," Chris said.

Kelly didn't appear too unhappy with the proposal.

"All right," she said and smiled. "Thanks, Grandpa."

"My pleasure. Maybe you and Allan would like to take a walk or something."

Allan rose and pulled out Kelly's chair for her. "I would enjoy looking at those prize-winning grapes I've been hearing so much about."

"Come on, Lassie," Chris said, gathering the dessert plates.

Lassie gave Chris only a quick glance. As much as she liked scrapings from the dinner plates, right now she was more interested in Kelly and Allan as they moved through the front room. When Allan opened the door and they walked out, Lassie quickly rose and loped after them.

Allan didn't appear interested in the grapes at all. He had a tight grip on Kelly's hand and they were walking off toward the pond. Lassie moved close behind them and wagged her tail, but they didn't seem to notice.

"So I reminded the judge," Allan said, "that in the case of Benson versus Carter Brown, February sixth, 1908, the decision had gone to the plaintiff."

"How interesting," Kelly murmured.

"Isn't it? The judge complimented me on digging it up. It saved my client twenty-two hundred dollars and thirty-three cents!"

"Imagine!"

Lassie glanced up at the strange note in Kelly's voice. Generally Kelly was a very down-to-earth person and didn't gush over things. But now she sounded like a starry-eyed teenager.

"Do you think so?" Allan said. "Well, let me tell you about another interesting case I dug up the other day. Parrish versus Hoag Plumbing Company. Now Parrish, a supplier, had secured for Hoag five hundred thousand feet of copper pipe and tubing."

"How interesting," Kelly said.

"The shipment was late in arriving and Hoag lost the contract because he didn't have the pipe."

"Wow!"

Lassie glanced up again at Kelly's exclamation, as if she knew that Kelly's enthusiasm about shipments of copper pipe and tubing was totally out of character.

Allan must have realized something because he looked as if he wished he could think of something different to talk about. In fact, he really looked like someone who didn't want to talk at all, but would have preferred to take Kelly in his arms and kiss her. And Kelly looked like that was exactly what she wanted him to do.

"Anyhow," Allan said in a voice half apologetic, "when the shipment finally arrived, Hoag refused delivery. Parrish claimed they were unable to make delivery due to an act of God."

"Heavens, what did they do?" Kelly asked.

They had stopped by the pond and Allan was looking at her with a dreamy expression. "What?" he asked.

"What did they do?" Kelly said again, her voice almost a whisper.

"What did who do?"

"Parrish and Hoag?"

Allan gazed at her as if hypnotized. "Your eyes are green," he said. "I thought they were blue."

The space between Allan and Kelly was no more than six inches, but Lassie quickly moved in and wagged her tail, forcing them apart.

Allan gave her a startled look, and the spell seemed to be broken. They both turned and moved toward the lawn swing in back of the house.

"You were saying?" Kelly asked in a choked voice. "About Parrish and Hoag?"

Allan cleared his throat. "Yes, well, the case went on to the Federal courts, where it was decided the altercation was not between Parrish and Hoag, but was Parrish and Hoag against the United States Postal Service."

"How interesting!"

"Well . . . yes. I mean, I thought it was."

They sat down on the lawn swing and Lassie quickly jumped up and squeezed between them.

"Lassie! What are you. . . ?"

Lassie licked at Kelly's face before she could go on, and she quickly turned away.

"Kelly!" Grandpa's voice boomed from somewhere in the house. "It's getting late and we've got a long day tomorrow."

"Yes, Grandpa."

They rose and Allan took her hand again as they moved around to the front of the house. Then he laughed and looked down. "Lassie, you make me feel as though I had a date with *you* tonight."

"Isn't it the truth?" Kelly said.

Lassie wagged her tail and trotted up the steps, ready to go inside. But Kelly didn't open the door. Lassie turned quickly, just in time to see Allan giving her a kiss.

Lassie moved fast, rising on her hind feet to give Allan's face a lick.

He backed away, suddenly grinning. "Yes, and goodnight to you too, Lassie."

"*Really*, Lassie!" Kelly exclaimed.

Grandpa was about to go up the stairs when Kelly and Lassie came inside. "Did you have a good time with what's-his-name?" he asked.

"*Allan*, Grandpa. It was very pleasant, but . . ." She gave Lassie a look of mock disgust. "Talk about chaperones!"

Grandpa laughed. "Well, Lassie is an old-fashioned girl. Goodnight, honey."

"Goodnight, Grandpa."

Lassie sat quietly and watched as Kelly moved around the room turning off the lights. Before Kelly drew the curtains she stood at the window for a minute and looked out at the stars. Then she suddenly knelt and gave Lassie a hug. "Oh, Lassie, do you like Allan? I do! But there was no need to act like you did. I don't need a chaperone at my age."

Lassie gave Kelly a consoling lick on the face, then followed her upstairs.

"Goodnight, Lassie," Kelly said, giving Lassie a final pat as she closed the door behind her.

Lassie hesitated a moment, then moved down the hall to Grandpa's bedroom where she opened the door and peered in. Grandpa was already asleep, probably dreaming about his big grape harvest. Lassie looked more closely, then moved to the foot of the bed. As he did almost every night, Grandpa had drawn the covers up to his chin, leaving both feet uncovered. Lassie grasped the blankets in her teeth and gently drew them down to the foot of the bed. She gave his exposed hand a final lick and closed the door behind her.

Chris' door was open. From the inside Lassie gave it a nudge, swinging it shut. Then she took her position under Chris' dangling hand and made herself comfortable.

She still couldn't remember the man who had left that scent. She rested her chin on the carpet and thought about it for awhile. Then she closed her eyes and drifted into sleep.

3

By six-thirty in the morning the first of the grapes were being unloaded at the presses. Out in the fields the pickers moved systematically along the vines, dropping the heavy grape clusters into plastic tubs. When the tubs were full they emptied them in the wagons parked at the edge of the vineyard. When the wagons were full, Kelly maneuvered the tractor into position and towed them down the hill to the presses.

Chris worked his own separate row. Lassie pulled a small red wagon alongside, and when no more grapes could be heaped into it, she headed down the slope to the winery where Clovis or Will Bradley relieved her of the burden.

Lassie didn't think much of the job. She enjoyed helping out, and at first it was fun trotting down the slope with the wagon rattling along behind her. But the work was dusty, and after ten or twelve trips it began to grow hot and monotonous. Chris helped her after that, pushing from behind to get over the deep ruts and soft sand.

"Chris," Grandpa finally said when they brought in a load, "you and Lassie have done just fine and I appreciate it. But Lassie looks a little tired to me. Why don't you take her off and play a while?"

"Well, I'm not tired, Grandpa. But if you think Lassie is, okay."

Kelly came roaring along in the tractor, the wagon behind her rattling and groaning under its load. She maneuvered the tractor through a tight turn and stopped abruptly, leaving the wagon in perfect position for unloading.

"Take it easy there, Kelly," Grandpa cautioned her. "If any of this equipment breaks down, we're in trouble."

She laughed and pushed the straw hat back on her head. "Oh, Grandpa, don't worry so."

"Huh! Only a darned fool could keep from worrying on a day like this."

"Chris!" Kelly called out as he and Lassie headed for the house, "there's a big pitcher of lemonade in the refrigerator."

"Hey, great!" Chris yelped, and headed off at a dead run.

Lassie didn't think much of lemonade. After Chris gave her a taste she turned back to her water bowl and almost emptied it. Then she stretched out and panted while she watched Chris start on his second big glass.

"What do you want to do, Lassie?" Chris asked.

Lassie gave him a single bark. letting him know anything was all right as long as she didn't have to pull that wagon anymore.

After he finished the lemonade, Chris went out the back door and walked down to the winery again. They watched Grandpa and Will Bradley operate the presses for awhile, and then Chris picked up a stick and threw it down the road. Lassie loped off, keeping her eyes fixed on the spot where the stick landed. When she had it between her teeth and started back, Chris was nowhere in sight.

It was a game they often played. Chris would

duck into the rows of grapevines and hide, sometimes squeezing in beneath the thick grape leaves
until he was completely hidden. Then it was Lassie's job to find him.

She trotted easily along the road, glancing into
each row as she passed. She finally stopped, sniffing the ground for Chris' fresh tracks. Then she
looked up sharply. About fifty yards along one of
the rows she had seen a movement; an unnatural
shaking of the grape leaves. She watched it for a
minute and then headed in, trotting fast along the
sandy earth.

She knew exactly where he was hiding. But she
trotted past, not even glancing at him, pretending
she was headed far down the row. Then, fifty feet
beyond his hiding place, she stopped and sat
down, watching behind her.

Chris couldn't hold it any longer. There was a
muffled giggle and then a laugh, and he groped his
way out of the vines. "Okay, Lassie," he said, "I
give up."

With her teeth still clamped over the stick, Lassie gave a muffled bark and trotted away. At the
end of the row she paused long enough to see that
Chris was coming after her, then she raced at full
speed down the narrow wagon road and ducked
back into the vineyard.

"I saw you, Lassie," Chris laughed as he came
running after her.

She squeezed through the foliage of some vines
and moved down the slope three or four rows, then
returned to the road. Seeing that Chris had turned
into the vineyard looking for her, she raced at full
speed down the wagon road again. When she was
almost at the bottom of the slope she ducked into
the vines and stopped. This time she dropped the
stick and stretched out, knowing it would take a
while for Chris to find her.

Several minutes passed while she listened to the footsteps and the rustling of grapevines. Then she could hear Chris' hard breathing as he moved along the row just above her. She listened, her ears pricked up, but for almost a minute there was dead silence. Then her heart leaped to her throat and she jumped to the side as Chris came bursting through the grape leaves just behind her.

"Aha!" he shouted and grabbed up the stick. He laughed and fell to his knees, wrestling her playfully to the ground. Lassie yelped happily and licked his face, admitting defeat. Then Chris dropped to his back and breathed deeply to catch his breath.

From far up the hill they could hear the muffled roar of the tractor and the sound of Grandpa's voice guiding Kelly into position. Lassie panted easily, watching Chris, waiting for him to get up and throw the stick again. Then her ears snapped up and she froze for a moment, listening.

Chris heard it too—the sound of a car coming slowly along the road next to the vineyard. He pulled himself to a sitting position and listened as the car stopped no more than fifty feet from them on the other side of the vines.

Chris started to get up, then hesitated as they heard two doors slam.

"This is it," a voice said.

With her head up and her ears cocked, Lassie sat perfectly still, listening. She knew that voice. It was deep and authoritative, and had an edge of meanness to it. She also knew it belonged to the same man who had been here yesterday. But like the scent, she still couldn't remember just exactly who it was. Deep in her throat Lassie issued a soft growl, warning Chris not to rise.

"What's the matter, Lassie?" Chris whispered.

Lassie glanced at him, then moved slowly and

silently along the grapevines to a closer position.
She stood rigidly alert, trying to see through the
foliage.

"It's a nice-looking piece of property," a second
man said. He sounded anxious to please the first
man—as if he might be an employee.

"Yes," the first man said. "I've been thinking
about this place for three years—ever since I
moved back to Colorado Springs. It's a perfect spot
to plant cabernet."

"But these are white grapes, aren't they?" the
second man asked.

"Yes, but I can tear them out easily enough. I've
already bought the property on the other side.
With those whites and this two hundred acres
planted in reds, I can build up a good inventory of
both."

The men were moving now, coming along the
vines in the next row. Lassie issued a low growl as
she followed, and Chris ducked lower, trying to
peer through the grapes. "Who are they, Lassie?
Can you hear what they're saying?"

Lassie could hear very well, but she paid no attention to Chris' question. As if expecting an at-
tack, she moved to Chris' side and held herself
tense, the low growl still sounding in her throat.

"You think Mitchell will sell?" the softer-voiced
man asked.

"He'll sell," the man said with a faint sneer.
"He'll sell because I'll pay his price."

The men stopped no more than six feet from
Lassie and Chris, their faces partially visible
through the heavy growth of leaves. The bigger
man picked a grape and ate it, squinting thoughtfully up the hill toward the winery. "This is a bad
time to talk to him," he said. "They're picking and
crushing now. We'll come back tonight."

The other man nodded and they moved back toward the car.

"What's wrong, Lassie?" Chris whispered. "Why don't you like those men?"

Lassie moved cautiously along the vines to the end of the row. Then she trotted up the slope to a small hill where she could get another look at the men. Chris was confused, but he followed along. When he reached the hill where Lassie had stopped he looked down. Then his eyes widened with surprise.

A uniformed chauffeur was standing next to a long black limousine, holding a back door open as the two men got in. The men were both dressed in suits and ties, and the older one had grayish hair and looked like a Senator or some kind of rich businessman.

"You know who they are, Lassie?" Chris asked.

Lassie knew. She remembered now, and a cold chill ran down her back as they watched the limousine turn around and drive off.

"I sure wish you could talk sometimes," Chris said. He watched the trail of dust rising until the big car reached the paved road. Then he headed down the hill and back toward the house.

Lassie followed, memories of the man in the limousine flooding back. She had been only a puppy when she lived in his home, and she didn't recall the man having hurt her in any way. But for some reason he was a threatening presence, and whenever he came into the kennels at the back of the house, Lassie's mother had always tensed and trembled a little and moved to the far corner of the enclosure. Lassie and the other puppies—her brothers and sisters—always sensed the fear and scrambled after her, keeping as far away from the man as they could. That was all Lassie could remember, and she only lived there a short while. But she knew her mother would not have reacted that way unless there was something dangerous about the man.

Lassie was uneasy. Should she try to warn Grandpa somehow? Or should she just keep out of the man's sight?

At supper Chris told about the two men, but Grandpa didn't seem concerned. "Probably tourists just wanting to take a closer look at the grapes," he said.

"But they were in a big limousine with a chauffeur, Grandpa, and Lassie growled all the time they were there."

Clovis glanced at Lassie and smiled. "You're a good girl for watching over the property, Lassie. But we don't mind people taking a taste of the grapes now and then. Maybe they'll turn out to be good customers."

Lassie barked, suggesting there was more to it than that. But that was the last anybody said about the subject.

After supper Lassie went outside and took a position in some tall grass down by the vineyards. From there she had a good view of the winery and the road leading up to the house. With her chin on the ground and her body almost hidden by the growth, she waited and watched.

It was almost dark when they came. Lassie spotted the limousine coming along the narrow road almost a mile away. She lifted her head and watched as it rolled smoothly along and turned onto their private road. When it came to a stop next to the winery she eased her head lower and growled softly as the chauffeur circled the car and opened the door.

It was the same two men. They stood by the car for a minute looking over the house and the winery, then the older man moved forward. Lassie quickly rose and made a broad circle around the car, moving into the shadows next to the storage shed. From there she had a clear view of the door to the winery. She ducked lower as the man knocked.

"If it can wait, don't interrupt me," Clovis shouted from inside the building.

Mr. Jamison pushed the door open and smiled. "Mr. Mitchell—Clovis, wasn't it?"

Lassie could see Grandpa working at a hand-operated basket-press a few feet inside the door. There was a look of surprise on his face as the two men entered. But then he frowned and turned back to his work. "Still is, Mr. Jamison," he said coldly.

Mr. Jamison didn't seem put off by the cool reception. With a broad smile he crossed the room and stuck out his hand. "This is my associate, Roger Finch," he said after Grandpa gave the hand a brief shake.

"How do you do?" Grandpa said. He nodded, then walked over and pushed the door shut.

Lassie came to her feet, alarmed for a moment. Then she turned and bounded around the corner of the building and raced up the steps. The door was unlocked and she quickly opened it enough to slip through.

Only half of the building had an upper floor. Lassie trotted through the tasting room and through a second door that led to a balcony overlooking the presses and settling tanks. She moved cautiously to the top of a staircase and eased down to a position where she could see through the guard railings.

Apparently Grandpa had given the two men a taste of wine. They were sipping from small glasses and remarking on the bouquet and the lightness of the taste. Then Mr. Jamison's face hardened a little and he set the empty glass aside.

"I can see you're busy," he said to Grandpa, "so

I'll come right to the point. I'd like to buy this property."

Grandpa's eyebrows lifted, then he shook his head and turned back to the press. "Sorry, Mr. Jamison, it's not for sale."

It was clear that Grandpa did not like the man any more than Lassie did, and that he was having a hard time being polite. But Mr. Jamison looked like the kind of man who didn't give up easily. He was still smiling as he watched Grandpa load more grapes into the press.

"Everything's for sale at some price, Clovis," he said, "and I'm prepared to make you a very handsome offer."

"This property isn't for sale at any price, Mr. Jamison. And I don't mean to be inhospitable, but we harvested today, and I'm very busy."

"I appreciate that, and I won't keep you more than a minute," Mr. Jamison said. Then he sighed, his voice suddenly warm and friendly. "Mr. Mitchell, you're getting along in years, and I happen to know that you have some notes coming due."

Grandpa turned sharply from the press, his face flushing with anger. "What about it?" he said.

"Now don't lose your cool," Mr. Jamison said quickly. "Hear me out. I'll pay off those notes, Mr. Mitchell, and I'll give you five hundred thousand dollars for your holdings."

Grandpa stared at Jamison as if the man were crazy. "Five hundred thousand? Why? You think there's oil on it?"

Jamison chuckled. "No, I'm pretty sure there isn't. It just happens that I want to grow cabernet, and this is an ideal spot for it."

Grandpa nodded. "Well, you're right there. The loam is perfect. Bale clay."

"Suppose I was to go higher than five hundred thousand?" Jamison asked.

Grandpa shook his head again. "It wouldn't make any difference what you went to. You're wasting your time."

"I'm not a man who takes no for an answer, Mr. Mitchell."

"This time you'll have to," Grandpa said and turned back to the press.

Jamison smiled, but there was no warmth in his voice as he gazed at Grandpa's back. "Nice of you to talk to us, Mr. Mitchell. I'm sorry you don't see things my way. Perhaps another time."

He turned for the door, but it suddenly burst open and Chris bounded into the room. "Oh! I'm sorry—I didn't know you had company, Grandpa. I'm looking for Lassie."

Lassie had come to her feet with Chris' abrupt entrance, and he quickly spotted her. "Come on down, Lassie," he shouted.

Lassie moved reluctantly down the stairs, trying to be as unobtrusive as possible. But she could see Mr. Jamison staring curiously at her. At the bottom she stopped, staying as far away from the man as possible. For some reason she found herself trembling, and a low growl came from her throat.

"Never mind, Lassie," Grandpa said.

Mr. Jamison was still staring at her. "That's a beautiful collie, Mr. Mitchell. One of the most beautiful I've ever seen."

Grandpa nodded. "Yes . . . well, she isn't for sale either."

"Of course not." Jamison moved across the room and knelt beside Lassie, lightly scratching her ears. She stood rigidly still, her muscles tensed and ready to run or defend herself if the man made a wrong move. She continued to growl softly, letting him know she had no intention of making friends.

"I had a dog like this once," Jamison said. "I

thought she was the greatest thing in the world."
He shifted his hand, scratching under Lassie's
neck, and she drew back a few inches. "What's all
the growling about, girl? I'm not going to hurt
you."

Chris moved over closer to Lassie. "Lassie saw
you walking across our property today," he said
defiantly. "She didn't like it."

Mr. Jamison smiled. "My dog wouldn't have
liked it either. Mr. Finch and I were just admiring
your fields."

Lassie edged back a few more inches, finally
getting out of the man's reach. Mr. Jamison rose.

The other man—Mr. Finch—hadn't said a
word since he came in. He stepped forward now,
holding out a card to Grandpa.

"In case you change your mind, Mr. Mitchell,
you can reach Mr. Jamison at this number in
Colorado Springs."

Grandpa stuck the card in his shirt pocket without looking at it.

"Goodnight," the man said, "and it was nice to
meet you, Mr. Mitchell."

Jamison was still staring at Lassie, his eyes
narrowed and thoughtful. He finally turned and
gave Grandpa a quick smile. "Goodnight, Mr. Mitchell."

"Goodnight," Clovis said, as if relieved that
they were finally going.

Lassie moved cautiously to the door and
watched, still growling deep in her throat as the
chauf____ ____ened the car door and the two men
got i____ ____re was something odd about the way Mr.
Jami____ ____d been staring at her—something men-
acin____ ____ondered if he recognized her.

"____ ____oesn't Lassie like that man?" Chris
aske____

____ndpa sounded tired when he answered. "He's

not very likable," he said. "Chris, you run along to bed. I'm spending the night out here. I've got the yeast mixtures to make up."

"Okay, Grandpa," Chris said, but he didn't move. The visit by the two men seemed to have upset his grandfather. Chris moved over to the press and gave him a goodnight kiss.

Clovis smiled, then eased down in a chair and pulled Chris closer. "Chris," he said after a minute. "That man offered us a great deal of money for this land—probably a lot more than it's worth if a person looked at it as a straight business proposition. But this land means a lot more to us than business and a way of earning a livelihood. I want you to have a special feeling about this land, Chris."

"Yes, Grandpa."

"Many years ago your great-great-grandfather bought our first vines from Europe and planted them on our hills with his own hands. When the time came for him to go, he asked to be buried in sight of those hills."

"Near the gate on the far side—where Mom and Dad sleep?"

"Yes, where your mom and dad sleep. Land like this is given in trust—with great love—from father to son. I know it's hard to understand now. But it's very important for you to know."

Chris could see that his grandfather's eyes were glistening. "Yes, Grandpa," he said.

"That man wanted to buy this land, Chris. But there is no price on something that is part of your soul."

"I understand, Grandpa."

Grandpa smiled and gave Chris a hug as he stood up. "I'm glad you do, Chris. Goodnight, Grandson. Goodnight, Lassie."

"Goodnight, Grandpa. And I'm glad you told the man no."

4

Roger Finch poured himself a cup of coffee from the silver urn on the coffee table. He stirred a dab of cream into it, then sat back in the soft leather chair and waited in silence.

The financial reports he had brought into the library were those of four corporations Mr. Jamison had contemplated buying in the last couple of months. The purchases would involve between twenty-five and thirty million dollars, and until three days ago Mr. Jamison had been completely absorbed in the complexities of the deal. If the timing was right, and certain pressures were exerted in the right places, it would be a financial coup with Mr. Jamison gaining control of almost a hundred million dollars' worth of mining property. But since they had returned to Colorado Springs from California, he had hardly shown any interest in the project.

"These figures all look good, Roger," he said as he thumbed through the papers. "Have you checked the stock-market prices today?"

"Yes, and there's not much activity. I don't think there will be a better time to start buying. And we should make the 'tender' offer on the Ketterling shares as quickly as possible."

Jamison nodded thoughtfully.

"Shall I give the brokers the go-ahead?"

Jamison thought about it for a minute, then rose and moved broodingly to the middle of the room.

The library was the largest room in the Jamison house. The walls were richly paneled in Phillipine mahogany; a fire crackled quietly in a marble fireplace, and a broad window displayed a breathtaking view of the Rocky Mountains a few miles to the west. But the focal point was the huge oil painting mounted over the fireplace. It was a picture of a beautiful collie dog standing in a grassy field, its glossy fur shimmering with highlights. Rather than the business problems Roger Finch had brought, it was the painting that now occupied Jamison's thoughts.

Finch was not surprised. Mr. Jamison had been in the dark, reflective mood ever since they had visited the Mitchell vineyards. On the plane coming back he hadn't said a word about it, but it was obviously on his mind. Edward Jamison was a man who usually got what he wanted—one way or another. Not that he necessarily broke the law to accomplish his ends. But he had broken hundreds of people, and when he was determined to get something, he usually found the weaknesses and soft spots that would enable him to pry it loose.

"It's an uncanny resemblance," Finch said, glancing at the painting.

Jamison looked at him for a moment, then studied the picture again. "You see it too, do you?"

"Yes," Finch admitted. "But of course all collies look more or less alike."

Jamison gave him a sharp glance, then nodded at the picture. "*That* one didn't. She took Best-of-Show and Best-of-Breed at Madison Square Garden three years in a row. She was international champion. She was also my best friend." Jamison smiled as he moved across the room. "She was the only girl I ever loved who didn't leave me or divorce me. And she never growled at me."

He sat down, suddenly reflective again. "I envy them that dog."

"Strange," Finch said quietly.

"What?"

"You can buy and sell almost anyone I can think of, and yet you want that old man's land, and even his dog. Why? Because he said no to you?"

"Not at all," Jamison said emphatically. "It's because Mitchell's got the best piece of wine-growing property in California, and maybe the best collie in the country."

Finch nodded, wishing the matter would get settled one way or another so Jamison could get back to business. "If Mitchell can't pay those notes that are coming due, he might be begging to sell in a few months."

Jamison considered it, then shook his head. "It looked like he was harvesting a good crop the other day. If he can convince the bankers of it, they might give him an extension on the loans. In the end it might break him but I'm not interested in waiting that long."

Finch smiled faintly. "You might find a way to get his land, but you'll never get his dog."

"Won't I?" Jamison rose and moved to the ornate desk at the end of the room. "Harry?" he said pressing an intercom button, "will you come up to the library? I have some questions about Lady McDuff's last litter of pups. Bring all the papers."

He returned to the center of the room and gazed at the painting until the man arrived with a stack of folders. They contained the complete history of the Jamison kennels.

The man left and Finch poured himself another cup of coffee while Jamison studied the records.

Finch wondered if there was really any chance of Jamison getting that dog. Even more he wondered why Jamison was so anxious to get it. It had been obvious the dog didn't like him. And taking a pet away from a boy the age of Mitchell's grandson seemed unnecessarily cruel. Or was the idea to use the dog as a bargaining lever to get Mitchell's vineyards?

Jamison seemed to have found what he wanted. Still studying a page of the records, he pulled a telephone closer and punched a series of numbers —enough to indicate a long-distance call. Then he eased back in the chair and smiled.

Edward Jamison could be very charming when it suited his purposes, and he turned it on now when his call was answered.

"Mrs. Haggerty?" he said, and then told the woman who was calling. After asking about her husband and children, he casually got to the point. "Mrs. Haggerty, you and your husband purchased one of the puppies from Lady McDuff's last litter. Do you still have the dog? . . . You do? . . . Oh, I see . . . Yes, well I'm sure she's a beauty, Mrs. Haggerty, and I'm delighted to hear how nicely you're all getting along. Yes, I'll be sure to drop in next time I'm out there. Goodbye."

He made five more calls, saying more or less the same thing. Then he tried unsuccessfully to find a man named Jack Sinclair. The telephone number in Glen Ellen, California, was no longer in service, and the forwarding number in Oregon also had been disconnected. The telephone operator had no additional forwarding numbers.

"No luck?" Finch asked when Jamison finally gave up.

To his surprise, Jamison smiled and slowly closed the folders. "Maybe the best possible luck," he said. He reached across to the intercom and thought for a minute before he pressed a button.

"Susan," he said, "I'm changing my schedule for tomorrow. I'll be going to California. Alert the pilots and arrange for the limousine to meet me at the Santa Rosa airport."

After he switched off the intercom he eased back and studied the oil painting again.

"About these reports," Finch said, "shall we go ahead with the project?"

Jamison looked at him as if not sure what Finch was talking about. Then he shook his head. "No. It can wait. I've got more important things to do first."

Clovis didn't notice the big black limousine turn into their dirt road. Chris and Lassie had gone off somewhere, and Clovis and Will Bradley were hosing out the plastic picking boxes and stacking them just inside the door of the winery.

The crop was turning out better than Clovis had hoped. With four days of harvesting, all the ripened grapes had been picked, and a good part of the juice was already in barrels beginning to ferment. Clovis had just finished cleaning the last box and was turning off the water when Will suddenly looked down the road. "Clovis?" he said.

"Well, wouldn't you know it," Clovis groaned, "just when it looked like such a nice day."

The car stopped and the chauffeur hurried around to open the door. But Jamison was already stepping out in his casual, self-confident manner. He was alone this time, a thin briefcase gripped loosely in his hand.

"I haven't changed my mind about selling," Clovis said and went on coiling the hose.

Jamison gave Will Bradley a glance, then came forward unhurriedly. "I'm not here about the vineyard," he said. "My business is personal, Mr. Mitchell."

"All right," Clovis said, "what is it?"

"It would be better if we talked privately."

There was something ominous in Jamison's voice; like a poker player who was holding a royal flush. Clovis frowned at him, then nodded. "You want to get started cleaning out those wagons, Will? I'll be back in a couple minutes." He motioned toward the winery. "We can talk in here."

Clovis moved through the door, then leaned against a table, his arms folded. He could not imagine what kind of personal business a rich man like Jamison could have with him. Whatever it was, Clovis didn't intend to waste more than two minutes with the man.

"How's your crushing coming along?" Jamison asked casually.

"You said you had personal business, Mr. Jamison."

Jamison paused as if undecided how to introduce the subject. Then he said evenly, "It's about your dog."

"My dog? What about her?"

"I think she's mine, Mr. Mitchell."

Clovis was so startled he couldn't believe it for a minute. It was either some kind of bad joke, or the man was crazy. "Are you serious?"

"I'm very serious, Mr. Mitchell. I am fairly certain that Lassie belongs to me."

"Mr. Jamison," Clovis said after a minute, "I've tried to keep cool with you, but I think I've had about all I can take. If you think you can walk in here and claim Lassie, you're just plain crazy."

Jamison lifted a calming hand. "Hear me out, Mitchell. If I'm wrong, I'll apologize. If I'm right, it will be very easy for you to check. I have the kennel records here."

Clovis felt his heart jump a few beats faster as

he watched the man click open his briefcase and bring out a manila folder full of papers. Was it possible?

"When I lived here about three and a half years ago," Jamison continued, and handed over some papers, "my dog, Lady McDuff, had a litter of collie pups. Six, to be exact. A few months later, she died."

Clovis took the papers, but didn't look at them. "What does that have to do with Lassie?"

"Five of those pups were sold," Jamison said. "And the sixth? There was a fire in our kennels one night and in the excitement someone left the gate open. That sixth puppy, who was only five and a half weeks old, wandered out and was lost. We presumed she was dead, but I am certain your dog was that puppy."

Clovis felt his heart drop. Lassie was about that age when they found her—and it had been three and a half years ago. "How can you be certain it was Lassie?" he asked.

"If she's mine," Jamison said quietly, "she'll have a tattoo mark in her right ear. The number is J-31."

Clovis took a deep breath, then turned away and gazed numbly out the window. They had had Lassie for almost six months before Chris noticed that tattoo mark on the inside of her ear. It had seemed curious, and at the time Clovis knew he should have made some effort to contact the kennel clubs, or someone who might understand the reason for the marking. But no one had come around looking for the lost puppy, and after six months Chris and Kelly were so attached to the dog he couldn't bear the thought of Lassie being taken away from them.

Clovis finally nodded, his voice thick. "There is a tattoo," he said.

Jamison said nothing, and Clovis thought

about that day three and a half years ago when he found Lassie. "I was inspecting some trees," he said hoarsely. "Down by the highway. I heard something crying. I got down on my hands and knees, and under the bushes I found this poor little creature. Drenched and starved." He closed his eyes for a moment and cleared his throat. "We sat up all night and fed her warm milk with an eyedropper. Chris was six then—Kelly just past fifteen. It was only a few weeks after their mother and father—my son and daughter-in-law—were killed in an automobile accident. I can't tell you what saving that little puppy meant to them. It was life in the midst of death."

"I'm sorry," Jamison said.

"Sorry?" Clovis turned and stared at the man. "That puppy had nothing to do with you, Jamison. She was something that came from God. She needed us, and we needed her. She's part of all our lives. She isn't yours. I don't care what kind of tattoo she has on her. She isn't yours!"

Jamison sighed and glanced at the folder in Clovis' hand. "I wish you would look at those kennel records, Mr. Mitchell."

"I don't care about kennel records," Clovis answered. "Legally that dog might be yours, but now she's a part of our family. You can't take away a boy's best friend, and take a dog away from the only home she's ever had. I can't believe anybody can be that cruel."

Jamison's eyes turned cold and hard and unfeeling. "I won't give up the chance to carry on the strain, Mr. Mitchell. If you force me, I'll go to the police and have them get her for me. I want her, Mr. Mitchell. Now."

"Mr. Jamison, I . . . . I'll give you every cent I have. But don't take Lassie away from the children."

"They'll get over it," Mitchell said. "And Lassie will have a good home. I take good care of my animals."

Clovis stared at him, realizing the man had no feelings or sense of decency. To Edward Jamison life was no more than a long series of cold-hearted deals and grabbing anything he could get away with. Talking to him about love or friendship or compassion was a waste of time. Clovis glanced at the papers, but they were nothing more than a blur of print and official seals. He finally set them aside and moved past Jamison, his frustration choking in his throat.

Neither Lassie nor Chris was anywhere in sight. Clovis moved past the limousine to a point between the winery and the house and stood silently for a minute. Was there anything he could do? Or would it just make things worse if he forced Jamison to go to the police? And how could he possibly explain it to Chris?

"Lassie!" he called out hoarsely. "Chris!"

There was no sound or movement and he shouted louder, almost hoping there would be no response.

Jamison was standing by the limousine, and Clovis shouted once again toward the fields. Then his heart sank as the porch door suddenly opened.

Kelly came down the steps, a puzzled look on her face. "What's wrong, Grandpa?"

"Do you know where Chris and Lassie are?"

Kelly frowned, looking from the limousine back to Clovis. "They were playing down below the last time I noticed."

"Suppose I come back about seven?" Jamison said from the car.

Clovis turned, a desperate note in his voice as he moved back toward the man. "Is there anything I can say—or do—to get you to change your mind?"

Jamison shook his head. "No. She's my property."

"Who is?" Kelly asked.

Clovis didn't respond; he couldn't. Jamison looked at both of them, then moved to the car. "Your grandfather will tell you," he said and slid into the back seat.

From under the porch where he and Lassie were watching, Chris didn't know what to think. Beside him, Lassie was trembling, her eyes following Jamison's every move.

From the minute the big limousine first appeared Lassie had acted strangely. She and Chris were on their way home at the time, and she had stopped dead in her tracks, growling and whining as they watched Grandpa and Mr. Jamison go into the winery. Then, when she and Chris reached the house, she lowered her head and tail and bolted under the porch. Chris had followed, wriggling through the gap of a broken board, and he had just reached her side when Grandpa came out the door and started calling them.

The funny sound in Grandpa's voice frightened him. And he couldn't understand why Mr. Jamison was still standing there, and why Grandpa wanted him and Lassie to come out. He felt guilty about not answering, but Lassie's low whimpering frightened him even more. And what did Mr. Jamison mean when he said, "She's my property?" Was he talking about Lassie? He couldn't mean that, Chris told himself as he watched the big car make a broad turn and start down the road. But his heart began to thud heavily against his ribs as he peered at Grandpa through the cracks in the boards.

When the car was finally out of sight, Lassie jumped to her feet and barked, her tail wagging again. Then she hurried across and squeezed through the gap.

Chris had an ominous feeling when he crawled out from under the porch. Lassie was happily wagging her tail and running back and forth between Grandpa and Kelly. But Grandpa's face looked even more drawn and troubled than before. "Why didn't you come when I called you?" he asked.

"We were under the porch," Chris answered lamely.

"I see."

"Didn't you hear your Grandpa?" Kelly demanded.

Chris didn't know what to say. Lassie barked and rubbed against Kelly's leg, but Grandpa was now gazing silently at the hills.

"Well, we were playing pretty hard," Chris finally answered.

"They didn't want to hear," Grandpa said quietly, "and I can't say as I blame them." He sighed heavily and moved toward the lawn swing. "Come on, I have to talk to all of you."

"I'm in the middle of fixing dinner, Grandpa," Kelly protested.

"And I have to put my bike away," Chris said.

Lassie lowered her head and started to move away, but Grandpa quickly grabbed her. "I'm sorry, Lassie, but it has to be done."

From the ominous sound of Grandpa's voice, Chris felt as if he would like to sneak away, too. But he knew he had to listen. He followed them all to the swing and sat down with Lassie and Kelly.

Grandpa looked even more miserable as he paced back and forth in front of them. "I don't know how to tell you this . . . except to come right out with it," he finally said. "The fact is . . ." He scratched his head, then looked at all of them. "The fact is, Lassie isn't ours."

Kelly blinked with disbelief. "Grandpa!"

Chris felt his heart stop beating for an instant. As much as he had told himself it couldn't be true, he knew that was the reason Mr. Jamison had come back. "Why?" he asked.

"She belongs to Mr. Jamison," Grandpa said quietly.

"She can't!" Chris protested. "Lassie is ours, Grandpa!"

Grandpa nodded. "Yes, we've always believed that, Chris. But you know those numbers tattooed in Lassie's ear we've always wondered about?"

Chris caught his breath. He hadn't thought about those numbers for years. "J-31?" he asked, "J for . . . Jamison?"

"I'm afraid so," Grandpa said grimly. "Jamison has his own number tattooed on every animal he breeds."

"You mean she's his?" Kelly asked indignantly, "and he's just getting around to looking for her now?!"

Grandpa nodded. "He thought the puppy was dead. That was three and a half years ago, and there wasn't any way we could have known. J-31 didn't mean anything to me."

Chris stared at him, feeling the tears form in his eyes. It didn't make any sense for them to have had Lassie ever since she was a tiny puppy, and then for someone to come along and say she didn't belong to them. It wasn't fair. And Lassie hated the man. Lassie lived with *them*, and Chris knew deep in his heart that she didn't want to go anywhere else.

"He can't have her!" Chris said defiantly. "We'll run away and hide where he won't ever find us!"

"Grandpa," Kelly said, "Are you sure he's telling the truth?"

"He's telling the truth, honey. He showed me the kennel records."

"Couldn't we buy her from him?"

Chris' hopes lifted for an instant, but were immediately shattered as Grandpa shook his head.

"I already offered him every cent I have in the bank," he said. "He wouldn't even talk about it."

"Lassie hates him, Grandpa," Chris said, "She runs away every time she sees him. She'll die if he takes her."

"Now, Chris . . ."

"If she isn't going to be in this family anymore," Chris blurted out, "I don't want to be in it either!" He didn't really mean it when he said it. But then he did mean it. Without Lassie they would no longer be a family. Chris suddenly felt that he didn't want to see anybody or ever talk to anybody in the world if Lassie was gone.

"Now try to understand, Chris," Grandpa said. "As terrible as it is, the tattoo proves that Lassie is Mr. Jamison's legal property. If we owned a puppy and somebody else found it, we would have the right to take it back. And no matter what we say or what we do, Mr. Jamison is going to get Lassie. So we've just got to face it. You have to understand that, Chris."

Chris didn't want to understand it. The tears suddenly welled up so fast he couldn't stop them, and he turned his face away and covered it. Then he jumped from the swing and ran.

He didn't care which direction he was going, and through the tears he saw only an endless blur of grapevines. He kept running, tripping over clods, sprawling to the ground. But he couldn't stop. He stumbled to his feet and kept going, the tears streaming freely down his face.

Lassie followed him. She ran fast enough to catch up, then she trotted along at his heels, silently waiting for him to exhaust himself.

Kelly knew it was as hard on Grandpa as it was for the rest of them; he too had tears in his eyes as he watched Chris and Lassie run through the vineyards. She rose and put her arm around his waist.

Clovis couldn't speak. He held her hand, squeezing it for a moment, then turned and headed for the winery.

Standing by herself, Kelly felt tears begin to clog her throat as she watched Chris and Lassie moving up the hill. Chris was walking now, stumbling blindly forward while Lassie tagged along, her head and tail down.

It wasn't fair. Lassie meant too much to Chris and her and Grandpa, and Mr. Jamison knew nothing more about her than the fact that she was a name and number on a list of puppies.

Feeling as though her heart were going to collapse like a punctured balloon, she finally turned and moved slowly back to the house.

Since their parents had died she had done her best to fill the role of a mother for Chris, and to keep the household going. Now she felt helpless, as if their whole world were falling apart and there was nothing any of them could do about it. She wished Allan were here. And more than anything in the world, she wished her mother and father had never been killed in that accident.

In the kitchen she closed her eyes and tried not to think about it. But the tears were in her nose and throat, and then pouring down her cheeks, and she turned quickly and ran for her bedroom.

5

After Chris had walked for almost a mile he dropped in the grass and buried his face. Lassie squeezed up close and licked his neck and hands, and Chris finally put his arm around her.

When they started back, Chris walked slowly and Lassie kept close to his side, and at the house they went in the front door without anybody seeing them. In his room, Chris stretched out on the bed and buried his head under the pillow.

An hour later Kelly knocked gently on the door. "Chris?" she called. When he didn't answer she opened the door. "Chris, come down and have some dinner."

The tears were still coming and he shook his head. "I can't . . . I can't swallow," he said from under the pillow.

Kelly understood. From the floor, Lassie gazed at her with sad, helpless eyes. "Lassie, you'd better come and eat," she said.

As if she were a hundred years old, Lassie moved slowly to the door and followed Kelly down. When she got to her heaping food bowl she sniffed and tasted a little, then lay down and watched Kelly and Grandpa.

"Chris isn't coming," Kelly said quietly.

Grandpa nodded, then bowed his head. "Thank Thee for the food on our table and . . . and help us

see the wisdom of Thy ways—which are mighty
obscure right now."

"Amen," Kelly said, almost in a whisper.

Clovis filled their soup bowls from the tureen
and they ate in silence.

"Isn't there anything we can do, Grandpa?"
Kelly finally asked.

Grandpa sighed and shook his head. "We
could probably refuse to give up Lassie, and fight
it in court. But that would take a long time, and I
don't think there is any chance of our winning.
Mr. Jamison has proof that Lassie belongs to
him, and there is nothing we can say except we
found her by the road. In the end he would get
her. And I think stretching it out that way would
only make it worse for all of us."

"It's like slavery, Grandpa. It seems like Lassie
should have some choice."

"Well, she's not a human being, and I guess the
law doesn't see dogs as nothing more than pieces
of property." Grandpa finished his soup and tried
to smile. "And maybe it won't be so bad for Lassie. I'm sure Mr. Jamison will feed her well and
take good care of her."

"Like another piece of his valuable property,"
Kelly said bitterly.

"Well . . ." Clovis shrugged and let it slide. He
knew Kelly was right. Edward Jamison was not
the kind of man who would love an animal or
give it any freedom. Lassie would just be something he could show off, and use to produce more
blue-ribbon puppies for the glory of Edward
Jamison. Clovis reached for the bowl of carrots,
then looked at Lassie. She had suddenly lifted her
head, listening.

Then Clovis and Kelly heard it; the quiet purr
of Jamison's limousine coming up the road. Lassie moved over to the table and pawed anxiously
at Clovis' leg.

"Lassie, it's a terrible thing," Clovis said, and hugged her face close to his. "I know you understand how we can't do anything about it."

"Oh, Lassie!" Kelly burst out and came around to hug her too. Lassie nuzzled against her, then drew back, looking in the direction of the road. Her head suddenly went down and she trotted off, heading for the stairs.

Clovis knew this would be the worst part of it, but it had to be done. Earlier in the afternoon he had found an old choker and leash in the winery storage room and brought them into the house. He got them now and moved wearily up the stairs.

Chris' door was locked and Lassie was scratching at it, whining anxiously. "I'm sorry, girl," Clovis said and slipped the choker over her neck. Lassie resisted, moving as slowly as possible, but Clovis finally maneuvered her down the stairs.

Kelly came along as Clovis slowly dragged Lassie to the front door. She gave Lassie one last tearful hug and then watched as they went down the steps.

Clovis kept himself going, his jaw tight to hold back the tears as he pulled Lassie to the car.

Jamison and the chauffeur were standing by the opened door and Clovis handed over the leash. Then he felt a piece of paper pressed into his hand.

"That's a check for your trouble," Jamison said, "I'll see that the boy gets a pup."

Clovis didn't hear him. He stood frozen on the spot, watching as Jamison and the chauffeur struggled to get Lassie into the back seat. Lassie was yelping and whining, pulling with all her strength to stay out of the car. Clovis wished for a minute that she would bite one of them, but he knew she wouldn't. She was too gentle to use her only effective weapon.

After the chauffeur finally lifted her back legs from the ground, the battle was over. Lassie was thrust inside and Jamison quickly jumped in behind her and slammed the door.

It finally hit Clovis; the realization that Jamison had thrust a check into his hand. He looked down at it for a moment, then crumpled it into a ball and threw it through the open window. Jamison gave him a surprised look. Then he seemed to shrug as the chauffeur started the car.

Lassie yelped and whined and pulled at the leash until the electric window silently closed off her last chance to escape.

"Good-bye, Lassie," Clovis whispered under his breath, and a moment later the car was rolling quietly down the road. For a minute Lassie's face appeared at the back window as if she was taking one last look at her home. Then the car turned and they were gone.

"Oh, Grandpa," Kelly choked as Clovis trudged in the door, "such a terrible day."

Clovis nodded, then looked up as Chris suddenly appeared at the top of the stairs. His face was twisted with torment, and tears were streaming down his cheeks.

"I hate you, Grandpa!" the boy cried out between his tears, "I'll hate you as long as I live."

Clovis stared at him, surprised and hurt. "Chris . . . try to understand."

"You sold my dog!" Chris blurted out. "You sold Lassie to Mr. Jamison!"

For a moment Clovis was too shocked to speak. He couldn't believe Chris could think such a thing. "Chris," he finally managed, "that isn't true!"

"It *is* true!" Chris shouted through the gush of new tears, "I *saw* you!" Then he turned and ran. An instant later his door slammed.

Clovis looked helplessly at Kelly. "What can I do?"

"He's only a little boy," Kelly said. "He didn't mean it, Grandpa."

Clovis was too tired and confused, and too heartbroken, to face any more problems that day. Nor did either he or Kelly feel like finishing dinner. Clovis helped clear the table, and after the dishes were done they both went to their rooms.

Chris was the first to go to sleep. Through sheer exhaustion and emotional numbness, his sobs finally gave way to unconsciousness. He lay face-down with his head under the pillow and his hand dangling over the side—nestled into Lassie's imagined fur.

For a long time before she slept, Kelly lay on her back, the tears standing in her eyes as she gazed vacantly at the ceiling. Crickets chirped softly outside, and somewhere in the distance a dog barked. But the house was silent and empty, as if all life had drained from it.

Clovis lay awake the longest. With his hands behind his head and the covers pulled up and exposing his bare feet, he silently asked for help. Only once before had he made such a prayerfully urgent plea. That was when his son and daughter-in-law were killed, and he prayed for help to carry Chris and Kelly through the terrible ordeal. That help had come in the form of a frightened little puppy he found by the road the next day.

Why was Lassie taken from them? Clovis couldn't understand it. But he wished that there might be some way to straighten everything out. Or at least make it a little easier for Chris to understand.

6

"There, my lady, is your mother, and all the trophies she won. What do you think?"

Lassie gave the painting and the trophies only a brief glance as Mr. Jamison held her with the tight leash. She was more interested in the big window and the distant mountains outside. Ever since she had been brought to Colorado Springs and the Jamison estate, she had been cooped up in a pen with nothing to look at but other pens.

"You're going to win just as many trophies for me," Mr. Jamison went on, "and we'll give you a better name than Lassie."

It didn't matter what he named her—Lassie had no intention of answering to it. And if it was at all possible to escape, she wasn't going to spend any more time in Colorado Springs than she had to.

He was pulling at her now, dragging her over to a big, ornate desk. From a drawer he brought out a heavy green collar with shiny brass studs and fastened it around her neck. Lassie tried to back away, but he tightened the leash until she almost choked.

"You'd better start getting used to it, and to me," he said. "You're mine now."

Still holding her with the leash, he sat down

behind the desk and gazed at her for a minute. Lassie gazed back, her eyes as cold and unfriendly. Living in this big house, with the soft carpets and all the gold-framed paintings and polished furniture, Jamison seemed like the loneliest, most miserable man in the world.

"Lambert," he suddenly said. He was leaning forward with his finger on a small button. "You want to come in here and get the dog? I think she could use a little exercise."

Lambert came into the library and took Lassie through a long hallway and finally out a back door. Lambert was the man who watched over the kennels, and he had been feeding Lassie the last four or five days. To Lassie's surprise he bent close to her and unhooked the leash, setting her free.

"There you are, Lassie girl. Have yourself a run if you want."

Lassie glanced quickly at the man, who was smiling down at her, and then moved cautiously away, glancing around.

There was a small golf course directly in front of her; two or three putting greens with small flags in the holes. Far to the left was a swimming pool, and to the right was a lily pond with a grove of trees behind it. Lassie trotted off toward the pond, moving easily as if doing nothing more than stretching her legs.

When she reached the pond she paused for a minute and glanced back. The man was still standing by the house, still smiling at her. She trotted on, following a concrete path that curved through the pond. Then she continued into the trees, moving a little faster once she was out of sight of the house.

There seemed to be a path leading through the woods. She followed it and a few minutes later

found herself on stone steps leading down a
broad slope. At the bottom she paused for a minute and looked around.

The woods were now thick with an under-
growth of ferns, and the path continued off to the
right. Lassie turned and followed it, gathering
speed, certain she was now free. Then, as the forest suddenly ended, she came to an abrupt halt.

Ten feet in front of her was a huge iron gate,
its closely spaced bars rising at least twelve feet
above her. To the left and right of the gate were
brick walls rising almost as high, and they
seemed to run off endlessly in both directions.

She moved closer to the gate and thrust her
nose under the lower cross-bar. But there was no
more than three inches of clearance. She rose and
pushed the gate, but it gave no more than an
inch. A heavy chain and padlock held it securely.

It now seemed clear why Mr. Lambert had unhooked her leash without worrying about it. She
was a prisoner, and they knew there was no way
for her to get out.

She knew it was probably hopeless, but she followed the wall for a quarter of a mile until it
reached the lower end of the property. There
were no breaks, nor were there any rocks or
heavy brush where she might climb high enough
to leap over. And from what she could see, the
wall enclosed all of the property behind the
house. She finally headed back, walking slowly
up the hill and to the edge of the golf course.

Mr. Jamison was standing on one of the putting greens with several dozen golf balls near his
feet. Lassie circled the green and lay down, her
chin resting across one of her paws as she
watched him.

"Well, did you have a nice run, Lassie?" he
asked. He hit one of the golf balls and then smiled
as it dropped into the cup.

Lassie turned and looked in the other direction. Mr. Lambert was still standing by the house, waiting patiently, the leash still dangling from his hand. On the left side of the house just past a Ping-Pong table, two gardeners were clipping the tall hedge that grew up against the brick wall. They were clipping near the top, standing on some scaffolding that was supported by two step-ladders. Lassie watched for awhile, then lifted her head as Mr. Finch suddenly appeared near the swimming pool. He was carrying a telephone, the wire trailing out behind him.

"Mr. Jamison, it's the real-estate agent in California," he said.

Mr. Jamison handed his golf club to Finch and took the phone. He listened for a minute, then smiled as he said a few words and hung up.

"I've got it, Roger," he announced with a grin.

"You mean Mitchell's selling?"

"No, the property on the other side of him. Now I'll squeeze them till they scream." He handed the phone back and glanced at Lassie. "And I've got the dog."

Lassie put her head back on her paw and closed her eyes, wondering what it all meant. Whatever it was, it didn't sound so good for Grandpa and Chris and Kelly.

"Lambert!" Mr. Jamison called out, "bring some food for me to give Lassie."

Lassie lifted her head and looked once more at the men clipping the hedge. They were working on the top now, cutting the foliage down to the level of the wall. Then she gazed at the Ping-Pong table only a few feet away from them.

Mr. Lambert arrived with a bowl of food and gave it to Mr. Jamison.

"Pick up these golf balls, will you, Lambert?" Jamison said and moved toward Lassie. "Here you are, Lassie, come on, girl."

Lassie rose to her feet and growled softly.

"Aren't you hungry, girl? This is ground sirloin. Not that cheap hamburger they probably gave you out in California."

Lassie backed off a little, then snarled threateningly.

Mr. Jamison didn't like it. He particularly didn't like it with the two gardeners looking on.

"You'll eat when you're hungry," he said confidently. He put the dish on the grass and studied Lassie with a cold look, as if realizing he had a harder job ahead of him than he first thought.

Lassie snarled again and suddenly Jamison was moving toward her, an angry look in his eyes. Lassie growled and turned away, trotting off toward the swimming pool. She had no intention of biting the man, but she didn't want him coming near her, either.

His face was red and he was striding after her now. "Lassie!" he commanded. "Sit! Stop!"

Lassie glanced back at him and circled the pool, keeping her lead. When he stopped, she moved a few steps farther and stopped next to the long handle of a pool-skimmer that was resting on the concrete apron.

"Stay right there, Lassie," Jamison said. "Don't move." There was a cold fury in his eyes as he came forward, his arms ready to grab her.

Lassie waited until the last second before she jumped. He was almost on her, his reaching hands less than a foot from her head when she leapt to the side. Then she took off at full speed, circling around the diving board to the far side of the pool.

For an instant she wasn't sure what had happened. As she raced away she heard a clanking sound from the metal handle of the pool-skimmer —then a brief cry from Mr. Jamison, and a heavy splash of water. When she skidded to a stop and looked back, Mr. Jamison was nowhere in sight. Then his head suddenly broke through the surface of the pool. His mouth was open, gasping for air; then he spit out a stream of water and pushed his hair out of his eyes.

Lassie stared at him for a minute, then looked off at the two gardeners who were hurriedly climbing down from the scaffolding.

"Are you all right, Mr. Jamison?" one of them shouted as they both came running.

"Get the dog!" Jamison screamed.

Both men stopped and stared at Lassie. She stared back, then moved cautiously to the side, making a broad circle.

"Here, doggie," one of the men said and moved closer. "Come on, doggie. Nice doggie, I won't hurt you."

Jamison was climbing out of the pool now. "Grab her, you idiot!" he shouted.

Lassie stopped, carefully watching the two men as they approached. They didn't seem anxious to come close to her, and she growled softly, letting them know it was not a good idea. But Mr. Jamison was out of the pool and striding toward them now.

Lassie knew it was risky, but this might be her last chance. She took a final glance at Mr. Jamison and took off at full speed for the Ping-Pong table.

"Stop her, you fools!" Mr. Jamison screamed.

She hardly touched the top of the table. With one bound she was on it, and then flying up to the scaffolding. There she steadied herself for a minute and glanced back. Mr. Jamison was shouting and running at full speed, the two gardeners loping along behind him. Lassie made certain her footing was firm on the scaffold plank, then leaped. Her front legs reached to the wall and she clawed at the hedge with her back feet until she was on top of the bricks.

There was a long drop on the other side, and nothing to break her fall. She moved along the wall a few feet, hesitating.

"Lassie!" Mr. Jamison shouted. He was on the scaffolding now, trying to reach out for her.

Lassie crouched as low as she could and jumped. The ground outside the wall sloped sharply downward. As she hit, she skidded and tumbled for a minute, then came shakily to her feet.

"You men!" Jamison shouted at the gardeners. "Get out there and catch her! Lambert—call Jeff and tell him to warm up the helicopter! Fast!"

Lassie was already moving, running at full speed into the dry culvert that paralleled the brick wall. The bottom of the culvert was strewn with sharp gravel that stung her feet, but she hardly noticed as she raced on.

Once she reached the end of the wall, she scampered out of the culvert and turned toward the mountains and the rising terrain that was almost solid rock.

An hour later she was several miles away from the Jamison estate and well into the foothills. There were fissures and pinnacles and narrow canyons that several times caused her to retrace her steps to reach higher ground. But she kept moving, panting heavily, her paws scraped and bleeding from the coarse rock.

Ten minutes later she heard it—the staccato popping of a helicopter motor as it approached rapidly from behind. She stopped for a minute, catching her breath, then scrambled to the top of a huge boulder and looked back.

They had seen her. The helicopter was coming directly at her and rapidly losing altitude. She leaped from the boulder and ran, dropping into a narrow culvert that might give her some cover. But there was very little brush, or anything else under which she could hide. There was nothing to do but run.

The helicopter was above her now, moving along at the same speed, its motor making a deafening clatter and its rotor blades swirling dust all around. Lassie slackened her pace a little and looked up.

A man stepped out of the door and suddenly he was dangling in some kind of harness a few feet under the machine. It was Mr. Lambert.

Lassie scrambled up the side and out of the culvert, then dropped into a deeper ravine, once more running at full speed through the boulders.

She realized it was hopeless. The helicopter swooped upward and moved over to her ravine with Mr. Lambert still dangling from his rope. Again they were almost directly above her.

Ahead of her the ravine was coming to a dead end, the sides now steep rock walls. Behind her, the helicopter was hovering low, dropping Mr. Lambert to the ground. Lassie eased her pace and finally came to a stop, looking around for some way she might possibly escape.

Mr. Lambert was on the ground now and unhooking his harness. "Just take it easy, Lassie," he said with a smile. "Nobody's going to hurt you."

Lassie moved up the ravine a little farther and paused. The canyon walls were even steeper here, and she could go on only twenty or thirty yards more. Overhead the helicopter was waiting patiently, the clattering softer now.

"Come on, Lassie, that's a good girl. Just stand still now."

Lassie stood still, her head lowered and her eyes alert as the man came closer. Then she opened her mouth and panted heavily, as if to show the man she was too tired to run anymore.

It seemed to give him confidence. "That's a good girl," he said with a smile. His hand came up, ready to grab her collar as he moved slowly forward.

Lassie waited until the hand was within inches of her neck. Then she ducked sharply, took a quick jump to the right and was past the man before he knew what happened.

"Lassie!" he cried out. By then she was fifty yards down the ravine and flying through the boulders again.

The helicopter responded immediately. The motor roared, and within seconds it was sailing along fifty feet over her head. Then it was easing down closer, edging out in front of her.

Lassie knew they were trying to scare her—to force her back up the ravine. The clattering of the rotor blades was deafening and the dust was swirling around her again. But she knew there was nothing they could do. She made a sharp turn up the side of the ravine and scampered down into the next one. Then she turned and once more headed toward the mountains.

The helicopter rose and made a broad circle, and Lassie suddenly saw Mr. Lambert again. He was standing on a high rock about a hundred yards to her left, waving his arms at the helicopter.

"Come back!" he shouted, "Come back, you idiots! Don't leave me out here! Come back!"

Lassie couldn't resist stopping for a minute to watch. She climbed to the top of a boulder and stretched out, panting heavily.

But the helicopter was not going back for Mr. Lambert. The pilot completed his turn and swept right past him, slowly climbing until he reached a position directly above Lassie.

She didn't move. The machine came down to within ten feet of her, the motor pounding and the rotors whipping dust in every direction. But the pilot could do no more than that; there was no possibility of his landing in the rough terrain.

Lassie finally jumped down from the boulder and trotted on, paying no attention to the thing. A half mile ahead she could see a grove of aspens, and once there she would have no trouble disappearing beneath the trees.

With the helicopter directly overhead, she ran at full speed over the last hundred yards. Then, as quickly as she entered the grove and was hidden from sight, she came to a quick stop.

Above her she could hear the helicopter moving on, keeping up the fast pace she had set. She moved a few yards more to a shady spot with a soft loam of old leaves and settled down, panting heavily to catch her breath.

The helicopter finally came back, moving slowly, making broad circles over the forest. Then it headed down the slope toward the spot where they had left Mr. Lambert.

Lassie listened carefully as the popping sound lingered over the lower slopes. Then, after four or five minutes, she finally heard it moving away, the sound fading into the distant valley.

For the time being, at least, she was safe. So what could she do now? She finally licked at her sore paws and listened for sounds of approaching helicopters. Then, feeling her strength returning, she rose and trotted on, picking her way through the trees and catching a few glimpses of the towering Rocky Mountains far ahead of her.

She knew that was the direction she had to go; toward the setting sun. But she had little idea how far it would be. In the plane coming east to Colorado Springs she had been locked in a cage and placed on the floor at the back of the cabin, unable to see out of the windows. But the flight had taken almost two hours, and she sensed that it was going to be a long, long trip on foot.

She turned left, once she came out of the trees. The mountains ahead rose too sharply to consider trying to climb them, and she could see a narrow road and what looked like some trailers and campers a few miles to the south. She loped down to the road, and keeping an eye out for Mr. Jamison's helicopter, she headed south.

It was a park of some sort—full of big trees, and dozens of people camping in tents and living in trailers. Lassie moved among them without anybody paying much attention. Then she stopped by a cluster of tents where a group of people were dipping food out of a big steaming pot. She edged up to within fifteen feet of the fire and sat down, waiting patiently.

They were eating the food from bowls, and it smelled delicious. Lassie stretched out and rested her chin in the dirt, looking from one to the other as the people emptied their bowls and returned to the pot for refills. Finally a man noticed her. He was bald-headed and wearing a shirt with big red and yellow flowers printed on it.

"Hello, boy," he said. "Who do you belong to?"

Lassie lifted her head and barked.

"You like chili, boy?"

Lassie barked again and moved to the man's side, wagging her tail.

"Okay," he said, "I hope it's not too hot for you." He placed his half-full bowl on the ground and Lassie gulped the chili without hesitating. It wasn't too hot, and there were good chunks of delicious meat in it.

A woman close to the fire laughed and filled up another bowl. "That's a girl, Fred." She came over and gave Lassie's head a good scratch, then put the bowl down. "You're a girl, aren't you. And a very beautiful girl."

Lassie gave her face a quick lick of appreciation and quickly finished off the second bowl.

Altogether she ate six bowls of chili and had her back scratched four or five times while she was doing it.

"Look at that beautiful collar," one of the women said. "You must have a nice master."

"Okay, girl," a man finally said, "you can go home now."

Lassie barked her appreciation and trotted off through the other campsites. At the lower end of the park she came to a narrow asphalt road heading south. The park probably would have been a good place to spend the night and get some breakfast in the morning. But she didn't want to risk staying that close to Mr. Jamison's place. And somewhere to the south the mountains might get lower and she could find a highway going west.

She walked alongside the road for an hour before it began to get dark. Occasionally she paused and watched the cars whip past, hoping one of them might stop and offer her a ride. But none of them did. People probably thought she lived somewhere in the area and was just going a short distance for a visit.

She was thinking about sleeping—looking off at the high weeds, considering where she might make herself a warm bed—when she saw the pick-up truck a couple hundred yards ahead. One of the rear wheels was jacked up and the driver was just removing a wheel with a flat tire when she noticed it. She kept moving, picking up her pace a little as she drew closer. Then, with the man busy tightening up the wheel bolts, she ducked into the weeds and hid.

It was possible, she supposed, that the man

might offer her a ride if she walked up and jumped in the rear of the truck. On the other hand, he might not like dogs. Or he might think she belonged to somebody in this area, and be afraid to take her.

Lassie watched as the man finally tossed the wheel with the flat tire into the back of the truck and lowered the jack. When he circled around and climbed into the cab, she moved cautiously out of the weeds. Then, with five quick steps and a jump, she landed softly on the truck bed. She kept herself low enough that the man couldn't see her through the back window, and a moment later they were pulling onto the road and roaring away.

There was an old piece of canvas at the front of the truck bed. Lassie clawed at it until it unfolded into a cushiony pad. Then she made herself comfortable, and with the steady jiggling and the pleasant whine of tires on pavement, she quickly fell asleep.

7

"Make the reward two thousand dollars," Jamison said. "I want fast action. And as soon as the posters are ready distribute them to every sheriff's office and police station you can—from here to California."

"Right," Finch answered. He took the papers Mr. Jamison held out and slid them into his briefcase.

Jamison picked up an eight-by-ten photograph of Lassie and gazed thoughtfully at it for a minute. After she had escaped late yesterday afternoon, he'd thought it would be easy to catch her. A nuisance, but certainly no great problem. Now he wasn't so sure.

When the helicopter came back with Lambert, he'd exploded with fury. Why hadn't they picked up Lambert again and flown him up to the grove of aspen where they had last seen Lassie? Why hadn't they landed somewhere up there and both men joined in the search? Why hadn't the pilot radioed for more help? Jamison could have rushed a dozen men up to that grove and had them searching within an hour.

They had finally done just that, and with flashlights and lanterns they had spent three hours combing the area. But Lassie must have left the grove as quickly as the helicopter flew off.

It was after midnight when they finally found some people who had seen her. About three miles away, a group of campers in North Cheyenne Park had fed her around six o'clock in the evening. They thought she belonged to one of the other camping groups in the park, and the last they'd seen her she was trotting away in the direction of the old Gold Camp Road. But there was no doubt about it being Lassie. They all remembered the green collar with the brass studs.

They had spent another couple of hours searching along Gold Camp Road, but they had found nothing. Which could mean Lassie had been sleeping somewhere off to the side of the road, or that somebody had picked her up and given her a ride.

It was the latter possibility that bothered Jamison. Someone who knew dogs might have realized that she was a champion and very valuable. Or someone might have just made friends with her, thinking she was abandoned. In either case, it compounded the problem of finding her, and opened up the possibility that she could be hundreds of miles away by now. Except that someone driving along the Gold Camp Road probably wasn't going too far. It was a narrow mountain road that climbed over a ten-thousand-foot pass to a town called Victor, and then headed south until it reached Highway 50. For anybody wanting to go east or west any distance, it would be a lot easier to take the expressway directly down to Highway 50.

With this in mind, Jamison had sent people to Victor and Cripple Creek and down to Florence and Canyon City to look around. But with every hour that passed, he knew the possibilities were greater for Lassie to be hundreds of miles away.

He finally handed the photograph to Finch. "Put the picture on the posters, too," he said. "And there's a complete description, along with the tattoo number on the back. Put the office phone number and your home phone number on it, and be sure to put the part about the green leather collar."

Finch nodded and slid the photograph into the briefcase. "Wouldn't it be better to put your phone number on it?"

"No. I don't want a lot of cranks calling here. If you get an authentic call, you'll get in touch with me."

"Mr. Jamison," Finch said hesitantly, "Mrs. Finch and I were planning to take our grandchildren to Central City this weekend for the celebration . . ."

Jamison gave him an impatient glance. "And I was going to Saudi Arabia. It looks as though we both have to change our plans."

"Yes, Mr. Jamison." Finch snapped his briefcase shut and shifted uneasily from one foot to the other until Jamison squinted up at him.

"What's the matter?"

"Well . . . Mr. Jamison, do you suppose that dog will try to get back to the Mitchell's house in California?"

"If she does, she'll end up right back here, and I'll guarantee you she won't get away again."

"Well . . . all things considered, maybe she'd be better off with the Mitchells. I mean she grew up with the Mitchell's boy, and I imagine . . ."

"What you imagine doesn't interest me at all, Finch. That dog belongs to me, and I'm going to use her to breed the best line of collies anybody in this country has ever seen. And if I have to keep her locked up in a cage to do it, that's exactly what I'll do."

"Yes, sir."

"Now get those posters out."

"This place is called Mt. Carmel Junction, lady," the man driving the pick-up truck said to Lassie. "It's called a junction because you can turn west here and go over to Zion National Park about ten or twelve miles that way. You even been there?"

Lassie looked off at the dry hills to the west, her ears cocked, her nose twitching.

"No, I don't suppose you ever have," the man said, and gave her a scratch on the neck. "Not if you live in Colorado. But we'll be heading back tomorrow morning, so don't worry about it. We'll have you home in no time."

Lassie had been unable to tell the man she didn't live in Colorado and that she had no desire to go back there. But as long as they continued traveling west it didn't worry her.

The man had found her early in the morning when he stopped in a city called Grand Junction to get his flat tire fixed. He had stopped earlier in the evening, only a short while after Lassie had jumped in the back of the truck. It was at somebody's house high in the mountains, and he had spent two or three hours inside, probably eating dinner with the people. When he came out a man and a woman stood in the door of the house and said good-bye to him. "Drive carefully, John," one said, "and say hello to Alice and Frank."

He had gotten in the truck without looking in the back, and they had driven all night without stopping. When he pulled into the gas station in Grand Junction, the first thing he did was reach for the flat tire in the back. Then he stood blinking at Lassie.

"Well, I'll be hanged! Where in the world did you come from? You been riding back there ever since I left Grandma's place back in Victor?"

Lassie had given him a friendly bark and the man scratched her neck and around her ears, talking all the time. "Well, I can't take you straight on home just now, lady," he said, "I gotta go clear over to the other side of Utah to a town called

Kanab. But I'll be coming right back after that. So if you don't mind a few days of driving I'll get you back home all right."

Lassie barked, informing him she didn't mind the driving—at least the part of it while he was headed west.

"Okay, lady, what's your name?"

Lassie gave him two quick barks knowing it didn't sound much like her name.

"Bow-Wow, is it? Okay, that's good enough for me."

After the tire was fixed he invited Lassie to sit up front with him, and they headed west again.

"My brother-in-law lives out there in Kanab," he told Lassie. "He's got a slick Ford pick-up truck he's selling me cheap. Almost new, it is. So we'll be coming back to Colorado in real style. Course I'll have to get rid of this old junk heap somewhere out there. Maybe just drive it out to a junkyard, huh?" He laughed and patted Lassie and she barked a response.

"I'll tell you what I'm gonna do, Bow-Wow. We'll stop for some breakfast and then I'm gonna pull off the road up here a ways and have a little nap for awhile, if you don't mind. It's not a good idea for a man to drive a long time without sleep, and some of these motels along here charge ten, fifteen dollars just to flop on a bed. But I think we can get comfortable on this seat here, don't you think?"

Lassie barked her approval.

After the man ate in a coffee shop, he brought out some bone along with a large paper cup filled with water. The man held the cup for her and Lassie finished it off, then chewed on the bones while the man pulled over to the side of the road and had his nap.

Lassie wished the man was going all the way to California. He was good company and seemed to enjoy having her along. But she knew this was the end of the line for her. That road going west from Mt. Carmel Junction was probably the one she should take.

When they reached the little town, the man pulled into the first gas station he came to and Lassie jumped out the door as quick as he opened it.

The man laughed. "You want to stretch your legs a little, Bow-Wow?"

Lassie barked and then sat watching him, glancing to the west as the man filled the tank. When he walked off to the rest room, Lassie stared at the closed door for a minute wishing she could thank him in some way, and let him know that he shouldn't worry about her. But she knew it was impossible.

She trotted off at a fast pace, glancing back a couple of times, and then ducked behind a small abandoned building fifty yards up the road.

When the man came back to his truck he looked around for a minute and checked inside the cab. "Come on, Bow-Wow," he called out. "We're leaving!"

Lassie felt terrible as she watched him go over and talk to the gas station attendant and then shout some more. But this was the only way.

The man circled the station and then stood out near the road calling for a couple more minutes. Finally he scratched his head and looked in both directions, then climbed back in the truck. He drove slowly for awhile, peering off to the sides and looking for her between buildings. Then he seemed to give it up. The truck steadily gained speed and finally disappeared over a hill.

A light rain fell in Glen Ellen that afternoon. It was not enough to damage any of the grapes still on the vines, but the dreary day seemed to compound the gloominess of the Mitchell house. After lunch Chris went to his room and didn't come out, and while Kelly washed the dishes and vacuumed the living room, Clovis walked up the hill in the drizzle.

He had thought things might get a little better as the days passed; that Chris would grow to accept the situation and find new interests. Instead they seemed to have grown worse.

Chris had apologized for accusing Clovis of selling Lassie, and Clovis explained about the check and how he had thrown it back into Jamison's limousine. But the explanation had done little to lift Chris' spirits. It seemed as if the boy had almost hoped some money *had* changed hands, and that Lassie might be recovered with another such transaction. Since then Chris had retreated into a numbed silence and refused to mention Lassie's name.

But Clovis had watched the boy wander through the vineyards, sometimes running as if Lassie were loping along behind. Other times he would climb one of the hills and stand for long periods looking off toward the east, as if expecting Lassie to come bounding across the fields at any minute.

Clovis didn't know what to do about it. With the soft rain dripping from the grapevines, he trudged up the hill and down the other side, and then followed a narrow ravine that would take him back toward the house. To the west the sky was brightening a little and he could see that the worst of the clouds were already passing.

He wondered if it would be worthwhile calling Jamison and asking one more time if he could buy Lassie back. But he knew what the answer would be. And he knew it might give Chris some false hopes if the boy heard about the call.

Earlier that day Clovis had heard that Jim Hanford, just to the east of the Mitchells, had sold his vineyard, and he wondered if Jamison had been the buyer. Hanford didn't know for sure, because the transaction had been handled by a real-estate agent in Santa Rosa, and the man had refused to reveal the name of the buyer. But the offer had been so good Hanford said he couldn't refuse it.

It sounded like Jamison. And if it was, it would be almost as big a blow as losing Lassie. The Hanford family had been growing grapes on that land for two generations, and Clovis couldn't imagine neighbors more friendly and helpful.

Clovis wondered what it was all coming to. Would the whole valley someday end up in the hands of rich people like Edward Jamison? That would mean the end of all the nice families, and probably the beginning of corporate farming. There would be caretakers for the vineyards, and everything would be done on a mass-production basis with nobody taking any personal interest in the land anymore.

And what would happen to him and Chris and Kelly? Would he end up in an old-folks home somewhere, with Chris and Kelly going their separate ways? Clovis couldn't bear to think about it anymore. From the ravine he trudged back to the house telling himself there had to be a silver lining somewhere. He just hoped Lassie was getting along all right, and that Jamison wasn't trying to teach her all that nonsense a dog had to learn to be shown off at those silly dog shows. He couldn't imagine anything more miserable for a free-spirited dog like Lassie.

The canyon was incredibly deep. Lassie moved cautiously to the edge and studied the rocky terrain directly below. The slope was almost vertical; a sheer drop of at least a thousand feet. At the bottom, a narrow asphalt road looked like a piece of black ribbon snaking westward. Somehow she had to get to that road.

After she left Mt. Carmel Junction, she had kept a good distance away from the highway. She had been lucky to get a ride this far west in the man's pick-up truck, but she had no doubts about Mr. Jamison continuing to search for her. So she had kept on a course parallel to the highway, always keeping it in sight, but never venturing closer than a quarter of a mile.

At first it appeared as if the highway only dipped out of sight for a short distance, and she had kept to the higher ground as she entered what must have been Zion National Park. But then the highway seemed to disappear completely and the terrain grew more rocky and difficult. Several times she was forced to double back and find another route to continue westward.

And then she had found herself among the huge rocky spires and columns, and nothing but solid rock beneath her. The colors were amazing as the setting sun cast giant shadows across the canyons. It was like a fairyland, with occasional pine trees growing out of the solid stone.

Several times she had traveled in a northerly direction in an effort to catch sight of the highway again. And then she finally saw it; the narrow ribbon a thousand feet below her.

For the third time now she moved away from the edge and trotted on, looking for some spot where she might go down. As before, she had to squeeze through narrow crevices and climb steep rockslides to make any progress. Then, after another fifteen minutes of scrambling and sliding, she had to work her way back to the rim of the canyon for another look.

This time she studied the area more closely. The side of the cliff didn't look quite so steep as before, and there seemed to be several rocky ledges where she might be able to stop on the way down. But it was getting dark now, and if she were going to do it she had to start quickly.

She took a final look, studying the rocks directly below her, then she stepped cautiously over the side with her front paws. Bits of gravel broke loose and went tumbling down, bouncing far out over the canyon. She held herself still for a minute and then slid forward inch by inch. Then she was dropping.

Dirt and gravel slid along with her as she skidded downward. The dust and sand provided no traction, and she crouched low, her legs stiff, trying to slow her momentum. Then, fifty feet below and several yards to the right, she spotted the first ledge. With the ground seeming to race faster beneath her, she scrambled as fast as she could to the right, and at the last instant heaved herself from the slide and made it to the narrow platform.

The next ledge was three hundred feet down, and on the other side of a long trough of loose shale and gravel. She moved to the side of the ledge and started down again, trying to angle across and not put too much weight on any of the rocks.

For a minute it seemed as if she were going to make it. She was skidding downward head-first, at the same time trying to scramble out of the flow as the rocks and gravel gathered momentum. But then everything beneath her seemed to be sliding faster, leaving nothing for support. She clawed desperately in an effort to get out of the rapidly growing cascade. Then she was whirled around and being battered from all sides by the flying rocks. She was tumbling, rolling, skidding and sliding; being swept straight down the side of the cliff.

Her fall ended with a heavy thud five hundred feet below the ledge she had been trying to reach. At the base of the cliff a pile of loose rock and gravel formed a broad, fan-shaped slope. When she struck it the wind burst from her lungs, and she was sent sprawling down another fifty feet of clattering shale.

At the bottom, she scrambled instantly to her feet, ready to move away from the slide and the possibility of any more rocks tumbling down on her. But a numbing pain shot through her left foot and leg and she stumbled forward, then hobbled away from the slide.

Blood was running freely from the paw and oozing into the dirt. She finally eased herself down and licked at it, at the same time looking around for any dangerous animals that might be lurking in the area.

She was still several hundred yards away from the highway. But the slope was gentler now, and covered with brush and patches of grass. She finally rose and tested the foot. Again the pain shot through her leg and up to her shoulder, and she limped forward with the paw held well above the ground.

There was water nearby. She could smell it, and from somewhere farther down the slope she could hear a faint trickling sound.

Every bone and muscle in her body seemed to be battered and bruised as she hobbled along. But she kept moving, past a sandy area with huge boulders and into a clump of green brush. On the other side of the brush she found herself at the edge of a broad pool.

She stood perfectly still for a minute, alert for the presence of other animals in the growing darkness. Then she hobbled forward and drank. She was not the only one who used the place as a watering hole. After she satisfied her thirst she sniffed the air and studied her surroundings, sorting out the various scents. Some of them seemed harmless; small rodents and birds and lizards. But she also smelled bigger animals, some that might not be so friendly.

From farther down she could hear the occasional whine of an automobile passing on the highway. But she didn't think she could make it that far. She had to rest first.

The paw was throbbing now, exploding with pain as she moved around the pond. A few yards back on a sandy beach, a high thicket looked like it would give her some protection. She hobbled into it and eased herself down in a grassy patch.

Once again she licked at the paw, but now her tongue was like sandpaper against the tenderly swollen area. She finally stretched out and quietly panted, feeling a weary numbness slowly enveloping her. When she rested her head on the ground, she tried to keep her eyes open and listen for any menacing sounds. But within minutes she was drifting into unconsciousness, the battered leg twitching fitfully.

She saw Chris running through the vineyards as if in slow motion, shouting happily, a look of wide-eyed joy on his face as he saw her coming down the side of the mountain. Behind him Kelly and Grandpa came out of the house and then they were also running and shouting. Lassie ran faster, but the distance between them didn't seem to grow any shorter, and she barked and yelped to let them know she was coming. Then everything seemed to dissolve into unrecognizable shapes and she suddenly felt a strong sense of danger.

Lassie came awake and brought her head up sharply, every muscle tensed and ready.

She could hear nothing over the soft trickle of water dropping into the nearby pond. But the strong scent of a dangerous animal was unmistakable. She came to her feet and stood perfectly still, the injured paw lightly touching the ground.

She realized now how long she had been sleeping. Deep in the canyon it was still chilly and gray, but the ridges high above her were bright with the early morning sunshine.

On the far side of the pond, birds were chirping and flitting among the trees, and from farther down she heard the roar of a diesel truck struggling up the grade. As silently as she could, she moved into the thicket and edged between two bushes to a point where she had a clear view of the area. Then she saw it—a full-grown male cougar standing on a ledge high above the pond.

It was a ferocious-looking beast; several hundred pounds of rippling muscles and razor-sharp fangs. As if it were the unchallenged ruler of the surrounding area, the animal gazed casually at the pool and the surrounding terrain. Then it moved easily to the side of the ledge and with several quick bounds made its way to the bottom. For a minute it stood perfectly still, sniffing the air. Then the head dropped and the eyes searched piercingly into the trees and thicket and the rocks beyond the pool. When it started forward the head was low and it moved in cautious silence, the muscles of the shoulders and back rippling with power.

Lassie knew the animal would see her at any moment. But there was no possibility of outrunning the big cat. Her only chance was to face it head-on, and hope to sink her teeth into some vital spot if it attacked.

With the cougar still coming toward the pond, she kept herself half hidden in the brush for another minute. Then, with her head high, she stepped confidently forward to the open sand, her gaze fixed coldly on the animal.

The cougar stopped instantly, its pale green eyes riveted on Lassie, assessing her, trying to calculate her intentions, expecting her to turn and run. But she made no move.

The cougar issued a low snarl and slowly came
forward again, its eyes now vertical slits of flashing red.

Lassie knew the worst thing she could do was
show fear. She took another step forward and
growled, her head lowered and her feet firmly
planted. The cougar was within ten feet of her
now, every muscle tensed, taking one slow step
at a time.

If they fought, Lassie knew she would last no
more than a few seconds against an animal as
strong and fast as the cougar. The big cat sur-
vived by killing, and every nerve and muscle in its
body was designed to make it more efficient at the
task. Her only chance was to bluff her way
through, to show no fear, and convince the animal
it would not come out of the battle unscathed.

Lassie had picked the spot: the soft white fur
between the cougar's chin and shoulders. With her
heart pounding and the adrenalin surging through
her body, she braced herself, her teeth bared, ready
to duck below the open claws and flashing
fangs.

Within five feet of her, the cougar suddenly
stopped, its tail twitching slowly from side to
side. For a full minute they regarded each other,
muscles tensed, both issuing low growls, the fur
on Lassie's neck now standing straight up. Then
Lassie lifted her head a fraction, suddenly uncertain about the animal's intentions.

The cougar's eyes had shifted slightly—no longer looking directly at her. They were focused on a
point just above her head, and then they were moving warily across to the left. Still growling softly,
the animal took a slow step backward, and for a
long minute it seemed to be studying the terrain at
the edge of the pool.

Lassie was uncertain if it was a diversion of

some sort, or if the big cat had really changed its mind. Then, as if Lassie no longer existed, the animal sniffed at the air and moved casually past her to the edge of the water.

Lassie's heart slid back into her chest, but she still didn't take any chances. She edged back into the thicket and cautiously kept her eyes on the big animal while it lapped up water. Finally, as if it didn't have a care in the world, the cougar turned and strolled quietly away, occasionally sniffing for tracks among the boulders. When it was finally out of sight, Lassie eased down in the grass and panted with relief.

She had almost forgotten about her injured paw. After waiting several more minutes to be sure the big cat was gone, she rose and limped to the edge of the pool where she dipped the paw in the icy water. She took a long drink and then licked at the wound, cleansing away as much of the dirt and dried blood as she could.

The ragged cut across the big pad of her foot was no longer bleeding. But it was still swollen, and it seemed even more tender than it was the night before. She rose and tried to walk, but it was like stepping on a sharp thorn every time her foot touched the ground. She finally drew it close to her body and limped away from the pool.

Following the tiny stream that trickled down the slope, she reached a spot where she could finally see the highway. With the paw throbbing again, she limped to the top of a boulder and rested.

She watched the highway for almost ten minutes before a car came along. It was a little yellow Volkswagen, flashing into sight as it weaved its way around the curves. Then it roared past and disappeared in the direction of Mt. Carmel Junction.

She knew it was dangerous to let people see her.

But with the injured paw, she couldn't possibly make her way through the rough canyon. She finally slid down from her perch and hobbled off toward the highway.

8

The two men had parked their battered van a short distance outside Mt. Carmel Junction the night before. When there was so much beautiful country around, it didn't make sense to pay money for space in a trailer park, or to shell out fifteen or twenty bucks for a couple of beds in a motel. And for them money was always a chronic problem.

The older of the two, Gus McGuire, was a stocky little Irishman with graying hair and a face that was deeply creased with smile and frown marks. Gus liked to think of himself as tough and seasoned and sharp; a man who had been around and knew how to handle himself. But beneath the hard exterior a smile was always waiting to show itself, and there weren't many things he took seriously.

In 1961 Gus managed a fighter named Kid O'Rourke, who was the number-two contender for the middleweight championship of the world. That was the closest Gus ever came to hitting the really big time. A couple of years later he had two featherweights, a middleweight and a light-heavyweight under contract and they were all good enough to make the preliminaries on the Saturday night cards. That was when Gus made the most money.

But it was a tough business, and there were a

lot of years when he piled up debts bigger than his income. So he had started handling wrestlers in the early seventies. He had the "Duke of Paducah," the "Mad Strangler of Zamboanga," "Gorilla Gorman," and a dozen others through the next five years. Of course that was all pure entertainment for the television cameras, instead of real wrestling, and after a while the television stations quit carrying the matches. That's when Gus teamed up with a mountain-sized wrestler named Elbert Albert Clayton and started touring the smaller towns out west.

Gus was amazed at the wide open spaces west of Chicago. For fifty-five years he had lived in smelly gyms and smoke-filled arenas, and he had no idea the mountains and prairies and deserts were so beautiful.

Elbert Albert, who was billed as "Appollo," also liked the wide open spaces. He had spent most of his life on a farm in Kentucky, and when Gus found him wandering around Chicago looking at the tall buildings, Elbert Albert had already seen as much of the big city as he cared to. Heading west sounded fine with him. As for wrestling, he didn't know much about it except for having wrestled a few contrary bulls on his daddy's farm. That was good enough for Gus. They headed west, and for a year and a half now they had been traveling from town to town with Elbert Albert taking on all comers, and Gus teaching him the fine points of gouging and kicking and scratching opponents without hurting them.

The night before coming up to Mt. Carmel Junction they had earned three hundred dollars for three matches in Tucson, Arizona, and the only thing Gus had lined up for sure was a Saturday night card in Leadville, Colorado.

So they had thick steaks that night. Gus barbecued a two-pound slab for Elbert Albert and a smaller piece for himself, and then he looked over a road map and suggested they drive through Zion National Park in the morning and then head north and on over into Colorado. Elbert Albert was agreeable. After supper they rolled in early, and they were up at dawn and had breakfast in a little diner just up the road. By seven they were headed west, the ancient van whimpering and sputtering along the highway at a top speed of forty miles an hour.

"Beautiful country, Elbert Albert," Gus said as they entered the canyon. "Look how the sunlight hits those rock formations up there. Makes them look like some kind of storybook castle, doesn't it?"

"Sure does," Elbert Albert answered. The seats of the van were not designed for massive bodies like Elbert Albert's. To look up at the cliffs he had to lower his head and curl forward close to the windshield.

Behind them a horn honked impatiently and Gus moved to the right as far as he could. The big gray car roared past them and sent shivers through the ancient van.

"Look at that." Gus smiled. "Those people'll go home and tell everybody they saw Zion National Park, and all they're seeing is a bunch of asphalt with a white line down the middle of it."

"They're going pretty fast," Elbert Albert agreed. Then he squinted hard at the road ahead. "Gus, look at that!"

"What?"

"Don't you see it on the side of the road? By those rocks up there."

By the time Gus saw it and hit the brakes, they had already gone past the rocks—and what looked like a big collie dog limping along the side of the road. Gus checked his rear-view mirror and backed

up thirty or forty feet. When they climbed out, the
dog stared uncertainly at them, its front paw held
a few inches above the ground.

"Hello, pal," Gus said. "What's the matter?"
He knelt in front of the dog and gave her head a
friendly scratch.

Lassie felt relieved the minute the two men
got out of the van. They obviously weren't the
kind of men Mr. Jamison would hire to search for
her, and they both had friendly faces.

"Fresh out of friends, huh?" Gus said, and re-
ceived a fast lick on his cheek. Then Lassie lifted
the injured foot.

Gus took the paw lightly in his hand and brushed
some of the dust and gravel away from the
wound. "Well, you stopped the right car, kid," he
said with a smile. "I'm an old hand at this. My
client here is a bundle of sprains, strains, twists
and cracks. You know how wrestlers are. I'm well
supplied with everything you need."

Elbert Albert seemed like a giant hovering over
Lassie. "What's wrong with the little fellow?" he
asked.

"Her foot pad is cut pretty bad, and I think she
might have a couple torn ligaments."

Elbert Albert smiled. "That's not so bad, kid.
They heal in no time, and Gus knows all about
things like that."

Lassie gave the big man a muffled bark, and
Gus brought a medical kit from the back of the
van.

"She's pretty," Elbert Albert said, "but she sure
could use a bath and a brushing, huh, Gussie?"

"First things first, Elbert Albert. Hold her
steady for me."

"Don't worry, little friend," Elbert Albert said.
He put an arm around Lassie and held her leg still,
"Gus won't hurt you more than necessary.

Gus soaked a cotton ball with peroxide and

worked gently at getting out the dirt and gravel. Then he put some ointment on another piece of cotton and taped it to the foot.

The peroxide stung a little, but the ointment felt cool and soothing. Then Gus probed the upper section of her leg and moved it back and forth while he felt the shoulder. Lassie winced from the pain.

"I know it hurts, kid, but I don't think it's too bad." He dug out an ace bandage and carefully wrapped the leg.

"Say," Elbert Albert said, "that's neat. I'll bet you could have been a vet."

"Sure, but how would you have done without me?"

"Badly," Elbert Albert said with a smile.

The leg ached, but felt more comfortable with the bandage. Lassie panted easily and watched while Gus opened a bottle of pills.

"What's that?" Elbert Albert asked.

"Aspirin for the pain. Open your mouth, kid."

Before Lassie could move, Gus grabbed her chin and thrust the tablet deep into her throat. She gagged and tried to work the pill out, but then she could feel it moving down.

"What are we going to do with her?" Elbert Albert asked.

Gus took the medicine kit back to the van. "Take a look at her collar. Maybe she has some kind of identification tag."

Elbert Albert moved the collar around Lassie's neck, but there were no tags.

"Nothing?" Gus asked. He placed a cereal bowl full of water in front of Lassie.

"Nope. What do you suppose she's doing out here all alone?"

"Maybe she jumped out of a car. I'll bet some little guy is crying his eyes out someplace."

"He sure ain't in view," Elbert Albert said.

Gus knelt down again and patted Lassie as he looked her over. "I had a dog once when I was a kid. Went everywhere I did. He never asked anything from anyone except to go along for the ride. And I always took him."

Lassie panted, looking from one to the other. The man named Gus rubbed his jaw for a minute, then stood up. "Put her in the van," he said.

The big man grinned. "You're in, kid," he said and reached down to pick her up.

"Be careful," Gus cautioned. "That leg's hurting."

Lassie couldn't have been happier. Ten minutes ago she had almost given up all hope of anybody picking her up. Now she was not only getting a ride, but from two men who were as friendly and helpful as they could be.

The big man got behind the wheel and the one called Gus put a blanket on a platform just behind the driver's seat. Once Lassie got herself comfortable and they were moving down the highway, Gus opened a can of beef stew and dumped it in the cereal bowl.

"It's not exactly steak, kid," he said, "but I don't suppose you're too particular right now."

Lassie wasn't at all particular, and the meal tasted delicious.

Gus watched her eat and then reached over behind Lassie and pulled out a banjo. "You like music, kid?" he asked while he tuned the instrument. "I wouldn't exactly say I'm an Eddie Peabody or Enrico Caruso, but no one has thrown any old shoes at me lately." Elbert Albert laughed and Gus slouched back with a foot on Lassie's platform. He strummed a few chords and then smiled as he sang:

"A little travelin' music makes the miles roll by, Travelin' music makes the hours fly . . ."

Lassie couldn't help being reminded of Grandpa

and the songs he made up while they were driving into Glen Ellen. In fact Gus and Grandpa seemed to have a lot of things in common. When Gus was halfway through the song, Lassie lifted her head and howled along with him. Then Elbert Albert joined in, and they all sang louder.

Through his big dark glasses, motorcycle-officer George Casey squinted curiously at the van coming out of the canyon. He was parked under a tree about three miles from the mouth of the canyon, a half-hidden spot from which he had a good view of the long straightaway down to the junction.

It was a favorite place for people to push their throttles to the floorboards. After all the winding roads in the park, a good many drivers like to make up the lost time, and nine times out of ten they would come barreling out of there at speeds fifteen or twenty miles an hour faster than the limit.

But the van hardly seemed to be moving, and it looked like the driver was waving one of his arms as if directing an orchestra. Then he reached down and switched on his radio as a sudden beeping sound interrupted his conjectures.

"Casey?" the sergeant's voice rattled from the little speaker. "We got an all-points bulletin on a lost collie dog with a green leather collar with brass studs. You seen anything like that around?"

"No," Casey answered, "I haven't seen any collie dogs. I've given out twenty speeding tickets; I've answered four malfunctioning burglar alarms; two traffic accidents; one trip to Emergency with a pregnant woman, and...."

"I'm not interested in your life story, Casey," the voice broke in impatiently. "Just find the dog. It's a priority."

"Priority? A collie dog?"

"I'll put it to you this way. The dog belongs to Mr. Edward Jamison, a very wealthy man who

lives in Colorado Springs. And it happens that Mr.
Edward Jamison and the Governor are very good
friends. The Governor would like very much for
Mr. Jamison to find his dog. Okay, Casey?"

"Yes, sir. I think I understand, sir."

Casey was still staring at the broken-down van
when he put the microphone back in its niche. A
dog? Where in the world was he supposed to find a
collie dog? He gave the starter a kick and the motorcycle roared to life as the van came to a stop at
the intersection just in front of him. From what
he could see, the driver was the only person in the
vehicle. He was a huge man and he seemed to be
singing to himself, still swinging his arm as he
looked both ways for oncoming traffic. Well,
there was no law against a man singing, Casey
supposed.

He watched the man make a turn and then he
shoved in the gearshift lever and let out the
clutch, roaring past the old clunker. A lost collie
dog! Huh, he thought. The chances against a collie
dog from Colorado Springs being in southwestern
Utah were about ten million to one. And the
chances of his coming anywhere near it were a
billion to one. He glanced in his rear-view mirror
just in time to see the little van disappear over the
horizon behind him.

Just to satisfy his curiosity he should have
stopped the guy, he reflected. But no, the Governor
had more important things for him to do. Suddenly
a millionaire's lost dog was more important than
keeping nuts off the highways.

Lassie didn't notice that Elbert Albert made a
sharp turn to the north, nor did she realize that
two hours later they were traveling almost directly east. After Gus had finished singing he had
stretched out on one of the beds in the rear, and

Lassie drifted into the first peaceful sleep she'd had in days.

At lunchtime they stopped under some trees next to a river and Lassie finished off a second can of stew. She tried walking, but the paw and leg were still sore, and Elbert Albert carried her down to the river for a drink. So she returned to her pad and slept the rest of the afternoon. When she awakened, the sun was going down and Gus was pulling the van into a thick grove of aspens.

"We can use that old tub back there," Elbert Albert was saying.

"If it's big enough," Gus answered. "And it'll be a lot easier if we can get close to the creek over there."

Lassie didn't know what they were talking about at first. But after they had spread out some tarps and sleeping bags and filled a big tub with water it came to her. A bath. She turned from where she was watching in the van and curled up once again on her platform.

"Come on, girl," Gus said, leaning in the door. "You still asleep there?"

Lassie kept her eyes shut, but it did no good. Elbert Albert finally came over and carried her to the tub and Gus removed the Ace bandage from her leg. She made no effort to help them. When she was placed in the water she sat in stiff silence and stared at Elbert Albert while Gus rubbed soap into her fur.

It was hard to figure out what Elbert Albert was doing. He had placed a tattered old mat on the ground near the van, and wearing just his pants and an undershirt he was going through all kinds of contortions; twisting his own leg, then turning a somersault and grabbing at his feet, then running a few steps and jumping into the air to land on his back. He finally stopped for a minute and looked at Gus and Lassie. "Don't forget to scrub behind her ears."

"No coaching from the sidelines, Elbert Albert," Gus answered.

Lassie turned her head away as Gus rubbed soap into her neck and started working the lather closer to her head. Once when Chris was giving her a bath, some of the soap spattered into her eyes and it burned like fire. After that Chris was always very careful, but she wasn't too certain about Gus.

"You know, Gus," Elbert Albert said, peering out from where his head was locked under his arm, "you remind me of my mother. She was always saying, 'Elbert Albert, don't forget your ears. Elbert Albert, are those fingernails clean? Elbert Albert, eat your spinach, or no ice cream.' She was a good woman—just like you."

Gus snorted. "Couldn't I remind you of your father?"

"No. My old man didn't care. He never looked at any fingernails. My mother was a nag, but she was a caring woman."

"Well, don't tell anyone else I remind you of your mother. They'll think I'm strange."

"I couldn't pay you no higher compliment, Gus."

He was being careful with the soap. He had lathered it up and under Lassie's chin, but he wasn't getting any into her mouth or eyes. She appreciated that.

"Okay, Elbert Albert, now I'll tell you what I want you to do. Lift the dog out carefully and stand her over on that rocky place."

Elbert Albert laughed. "Okay, Moms." He came over and lifted her from the tub, holding her well away from him as he carried her to the rocks.

"One more crack like that, and you'll be hunting for a new manager," Gus said.

"I was only funning."

"Well, knock it off."

"Sure, Mr. McGuire."

Gus gave him a sour look. "Get that pot of water and pour it over her while I hold her."

"Anything you say, Mr. McGuire."

Lassie watched closely and then felt a little relief as Gus tested the water to make sure it wasn't too hot. She stood perfectly still as it came pouring over her head and washed down her back. Then she gave herself a good shake, spraying the water off in all directions. The two men backed away and Gus went for some towels.

"Listen, kid," Elbert Albert said, "You're not only going to feel great when Gus gets through, you're going to be a knockout."

"She hates me right now," Gus said.

"Well, no one likes soap and water. It isn't natural."

Lassie looked at Elbert Albert and panted, showing she agreed with that one hundred percent.

"I've been thinking about a name for her," Elbert Albert said. "How about Violet?"

Gus looked at him and groaned. "No, Elbert Albert."

"I knew a great Violet once."

"And I knew a great Bombelina. But we're not calling her that, either."

"We have to call her something.

Gus stepped back and took a long look at her. "How about Lady?"

"Well, it's kind of classy. But why not? She's a classy-looking girl."

Lassie gave Gus a broad lick on the face as he finished drying her. The name was not as good as Lassie, but it was certainly better than Violet. It was also better than Bow-Wow or Bombelina.

"I don't know where you've been or where you were going," Gus said to her, "but it's a real pleasure knowing you."

Lassie did feel a hundred percent better. With

all the dust and burs and twigs she had accumu-
lated she had begun to itch and feel like an old
desert burro. Now her skin tingled and her long
fur was once again smooth and silky. She shook
herself pleasurably and wagged her tail. But her
attempt to dance around was cut short the minute
she touched the sore paw to the ground.

"Okay, just hang on there a minute," Gus said,
"We'll get those bandages back on."

When he finished the doctoring, Gus brought out
a small barbecue grill and cooked steaks for all of
them. Then Gus and Elbert Albert washed the
dishes, and Lassie hobbled around the campsite,
doing some exploring.

Something was wrong, she decided. The sun
seemed to be going down a little earlier than it
should. And for some reason the country around
her looked familiar. She finally realized what it
was. She had been in this area before—when she
was coming west with the man in the pick-up
truck. The high mountains with the snow-capped
peaks were only a short distance to the east, and
this was near the place where the man had his
tire fixed.

Lassie came back to the campsite uncertain what
to do. Her leg and paw were in no condition to do
any long-distance walking. And even if she could,
it might be dangerous for her to be seen around
here.

"What's the matter, Lady?" Gus asked. He had
his banjo out again and he was sitting with his
back against the van. "Don't you like being all
nice and clean?"

Lassie moved to his side where she nudged his
arm and gave his face a lick. The best thing, she
decided, was to stick with Gus and Elbert Albert.
Short of being home she couldn't imagine nicer
people to be with. And maybe sometime later they
would be heading west again. From the looks of

things, Gus and Elbert Albert did quite a bit of traveling.

"What would you like to hear, Lady?"

Lassie stretched out and looked at him. What she would like to hear was Grandpa singing, "That Hometown Feeling." But she didn't suppose Gus knew that song.

9

Chris knew it was going to be the worst day of his life. He didn't want to get out of bed, and the last thing he wanted to do was stand outside the house and wait for the schoolbus without Lassie beside him.

He didn't know why he hated the idea so much. But having a dog like Lassie had been the thing that always brought him a little respect from the other kids. He was a little smaller than most of the other boys, so he couldn't hit a baseball as far, or run as fast, or act as tough around the girls. But having Lassie had always made up for those deficiencies. When the bus pulled up every morning and all the kids looked out the windows and shouted and whistled to get Lassie's attention, Chris always felt a flush of pride. He knew the others were a little envious of him. But now he had nothing.

"You'd better hurry, Chris!" Kelly shouted from the bottom of the stairs.

"Okay," he answered and pulled himself slowly out of bed.

He washed and put on the new clothes Kelly had bought for him the day before, then trudged down to the breakfast table.

"Say, you're looking mighty handsome," Grandpa said. He had already finished breakfast and was heading out the back door. "Have a good day, Chris."

The door banged shut and Kelly brought him half a grapefruit and a plate of scrambled eggs and bacon.

"Don't look so glum, Chris. It always seems much worse than it is when you start a new year at school. And all the kids seem to like Miss Kramer."

"Yeah," Chris murmured. When the school term ended last June, he was looking forward to September and being in Miss Kramer's class. But he had Lassie then.

Chris wondered about something he had overheard Allan Fogerty say to Kelly last night. Allan had come over for dinner, and afterwards, when Chris was sent up to have a bath and get ready for school in the morning, he had sat on the stairs for awhile, feeling depressed and wondering about Lassie.

In the kitchen Kelly was telling Allan the whole story again; about how Mr. Jamison came to the house wanting to buy the vineyards, and then returning a couple of days later to say Lassie belonged to him.

"Did Jamison show the kennel papers to your grandfather?" Allan had asked.

"Yes, he did."

There was a long silence after that, and Chris could hear Allan putting plates away in the cupboard. "I wish your grandfather had called me before he turned Lassie over," Allan finally said.

"You couldn't have done anything," Kelly answered. "She's Jamison's dog. She has his tattoo in her ear."

"Just the same, I'd like to have a look at Jamison's records." A cupboard door closed and Allan sounded thoughtful. "I think I'll go down to the winery and talk to your grandfather."

"Don't, Allan," Kelly said quickly. "It's all over. She's his. Please let's not talk about it anymore."

That was the end of the conversation, and Chris had thought about it all through his bath, wishing Kelly had let Allan look over the papers.

He wondered again about it as he ate his breakfast. Maybe there was something wrong with the papers. Maybe Mr. Jamison made up the whole thing about Lassie being his. Except the tattoo was there.

Chris knew miracles didn't happen, and he would probably never see Lassie again. But every night since Mr. Jamison had taken her he had said his prayers faithfully. He prayed that Lassie would run away and be taken care of wherever she was.

"The bus will be here any minute," Kelly warned him.

Chris got his notebook and new pencils from where he had left them on the dining room table. When he came through the kitchen and headed for the back door Kelly smiled at him. "It's going to be all right once you see your old friends again," she said.

Chris nodded and went out. It was a little chilly outside and he could see the bus rocking and swaying as it came slowly up the road. He went on out to the gate, but then stayed behind it hoping nobody would notice Lassie's absence.

"Chris!" Grandpa called out from the winery door, "have a happy first day at school."

Chris nodded to him and turned back to the approaching bus. Then the back door slammed and Kelly hurried out. "You forgot your lunch, Chris."

When she brought him the lunch box she opened the gate for him. "What's the matter?" she asked.

Chris suddenly felt so lonely he wanted to cry. "I never went to school before without Lassie waiting here with me."

Kelly suddenly knelt beside him. "Oh, Chris, honey, don't think about it. You'll just make yourself sick."

The bus was squealing to a stop now and all the kids were hanging out the windows. Chris moved through the gate and headed for the front door of the bus.

"Hey, where's Lassie?" somebody shouted.

"Is Lassie sick?" somebody else asked. "How come Lassie's not here, Chris?"

Chris felt as if his heart had dropped to the bottom of his stomach. He trudged on to the door and looked back at Kelly.

"Kids, we don't have Lassie anymore," she said.

"Why not, Kelly?" somebody asked.

Chris climbed the steps and found everybody staring at him as he dropped into the first empty seat.

"Gee, what happened, Chris?" the boy next to him asked.

Even Mr. Kernen, the bus driver, was twisted around to hear Chris' answer.

"A man named Mr. Jamison came and said Lassie belonged to him," Chris said. "He had a bunch of papers and things to prove it, so we had to give her to him." Once it was out, he clamped his teeth together to hold back the tears.

"Isn't that the mean old guy who used to live on the other side of the valley?" somebody behind him asked.

"Yeah," somebody else said from the other side. "He's the guy who wouldn't ever let anybody walk across his property."

"And remember at Halloween, he'd never give anybody any treats. He always had that man standing out in front of his place with a shotgun."

"Boy!" somebody else said. "And now he took Lassie!"

Chris couldn't hold back the tears. He kept his

head up and stared straight ahead, but his eyes suddenly blurred and the tears trickled slowly down his cheeks and nose.

Mr. Kernen quietly shut the door and they all headed for school in silence.

It was a much more pleasant morning for Lassie. Her leg and paw felt a hundred percent better, and after breakfast Gus rewrapped the Ace bandage so she could walk more easily.

"Okay, Elbert Albert," he said when the van was all loaded up, "time for some road work."

"Aw, Gus," Elbert Albert groaned. He was about to slide behind the wheel and start driving.

"Nope," Gus said firmly. "We skipped yesterday morning, but you've got to keep in shape. Get your sweatsuit on."

Elbert Albert went to the back of the van and Gus took a hard look at Lassie. "And it wouldn't hurt you to give that leg a little exercise too, Lady. How about it?"

Lassie barked, agreeing with him.

They didn't go back to the main highway. Gus drove the van along a narrow, graveled road that followed the river, and Elbert Albert and Lassie jogged alongside while Gus hung out the window and watched.

Once she was moving, Lassie's leg felt a lot better. But after a mile or so, Gus insisted she get back in the van while Elbert Albert continued jogging. Elbert Albert sniffed and skipped and jumped around, and acted as if he were punching at things all the time he ran.

"Come on," Gus urged him, "Just half an hour more and then we'll get started for Leadville."

"Do we have to go to Leadville?" Elbert Albert panted.

"We have an almost guarantee for tomorrow night."

Elbert Albert punched a few more imaginary opponents, then glanced at the mountains. "I wish we could stay out here like this all the time, Gus—you and me and Lady."

"And give up eating?"

"Some people live on nuts and berries."

"You and Lady don't. In fact I notice both of you eat more than your fair share of good red meat."

"Maybe we could adjust," Elbert Albert said and squinted over at him. "Gus, does it ever occur to you I'm never going to be champion?"

"No," Gus answered emphatically. "You're going to get your big break any year now. In fact I've been writing to a lot of people in New York and Chicago and I wouldn't be surprised if there was a telegram one of these days telling us to come to Madison Square Garden as fast as we can."

"I ain't getting any younger, Gus."

"Neither is anyone else. You're a slow ripener. But when you get there, you're going to be great."

"It's nice of you to say so, but I ain't got no class, Gus."

Gus gave him an impatient look. "Who wants a wrestler with class? I want a wrestler who knows how to take falls, and make the audience think he's getting killed or murdering the other guy. You're great at that. You try to get class and you'll blow the whole act."

"You know what class is, Gus?" He glanced past Gus to where Lassie was looking through the windshield. "She's class."

"So now what are you telling me—you want to be a collie dog?"

Elbert Albert smiled. "Maybe I do. You've been great to me, and I sure would like you to have a winner, Gus."

"Okay, that's enough," Gus said. He brought the van to a stop.

Lassie went back to her platform, Elbert Albert

got in and they started driving east again. She had no idea where Leadville might be, but through the next two or three hours it seemed like they were climbing higher and higher into the mountains.

Gus finally stopped in a small mountain town to do some shopping. Then they drove on for a few miles before he pulled off to the side. "Lunchtime," he said.

They were in a beautiful spot, high in the Rocky Mountains with a river cutting through a gorge far below them. The air was thin and clear, and rising all around were towering peaks that still had patches of snow.

"Hey, my favorite! Submarine sandwiches!" Elbert Albert exclaimed when Gus spread out a blanket and opened the brown bag. "Did you get one for Lady?"

"No. Lady gets chopped sirloin." He unwrapped a white package and scraped the meat into a bowl for Lassie.

"Hey, you rate, kid," Elbert Albert said.

"She's the prettiest girl in the state," Gus said.

Elbert Albert took a big bite of his sandwich and watched Lassie eat. "You know, Gus, she's the kind of a dog that makes you feel you should be eating on a tablecloth. You know what I mean? I really love her."

Gus shook his head. "That's all I need! A love-sick wrestler, and a dog that wants to eat on a tablecloth. Come on, shape up!"

"What if she belongs to somebody?" Elbert Albert asked. "I mean what if there's some kid crying his eyes out somewhere, and walking around shouting for her to come home? That's real sad, Gus."

Lassie was stretched out on the blanket with her chin between her paws, looking from one of them to the other as they talked.

"Then how come the kid left her in Zion Canyon with her leg all banged up?"

"Maybe it was somebody camping there and the dog wandered off and got herself banged up?"

"Then the people would have been around there looking for her, wouldn't they? And we didn't see any cars for miles around."

Elbert Albert thought it over and nodded. "Yeah. I guess you're right. But it doesn't seem like anybody would put a nice collar like that on her if they didn't want her anymore."

Lassie wondered what they would think about the man who put that collar on her. Gus and Elbert Albert were certainly nothing like Mr. Jamison. But if he found them all together and showed them the papers he'd shown Grandpa, they would probably hand her over. Apparently nobody could do anything about those papers. And no matter what Lassie wanted, the papers gave Mr. Jamison the right to do whatever he wanted with her.

Lassie took a nap when they started again. In the passenger seat beside her, Gus also dozed a little, and he didn't seem to notice when the sound of a helicopter suddenly came to Lassie's ears. She quickly lifted her head and listened, then looked at Elbert Albert as he leaned forward over the steering wheel and peered up.

"What's the matter?" Gus asked, suddenly coming awake.

"Helicopter," Elbert Albert answered. "Ain't the cops, either."

Lassie stepped down from the platform and moved to the rear of the van where she could see out the back window.

She recognized the helicopter immediately—the same one that had chased her through the rocky hills behind Jamison's house. It was coming down lower now, as if the two men inside were trying to get a closer look at the van. Lassie quickly backed away from the window and squeezed in among the sleeping bags and bedding.

"Whad'ya suppose they're up to?" Gus said. He slid into the seat next to Elbert Albert and rolled down the side window. "Hello!" he shouted, and waved at the men.

About ten seconds passed while the machine hovered over them. Then it suddenly rose and swooped away.

Lassie returned to the window and watched as the helicopter seemed to be chasing after a pick-up truck that was going in the opposite direction. In the rear of the truck a golden Labrador retriever was lying on a bunch of feed sacks, staring up at the machine.

Lassie felt relieved as both the helicopter and the truck disappeared around a hill. But it was clear that Mr. Jamison was still searching for her, and she probably wouldn't be safe for a long while.

"Well, that's the most peculiar thing I ever saw," Gus said and rolled his window back up.

Elbert Albert grinned. "Maybe they're looking for us—wanting us to hurry back to Madison Square Garden."

"Huh!" Gus snorted. He made himself comfortable and closed his eyes again. "It'll happen, Elbert Albert, it'll happen."

Lassie liked the town of Leadville. They arrived after dark that night and she couldn't see much of the place. But the next morning she was up at dawn and she slipped out an open window of the van and did some exploring while Gus and Elbert Albert were still sleeping.

They had camped about two miles from town, up on an aspen-covered slope at the end of a dirt road. From there she had a good view of the entire valley and the encircling snow-capped peaks. The whole valley was extremely high; the air was thin and chilly and a light frost covered everything in sight.

Lassie trotted off along the side of the slope,

sniffing, keeping alert for any animals that might give her trouble. Then she stopped at the edge of a canyon that ran higher into the mountains.

There were a number of odd-looking structures scattered along the gulch—rusty sheds that looked a hundred years old, and a number of deep holes with huge piles of gray dirt standing next to them. Lassie cautiously approached one of them and sniffed around the shed, then peered into the hole. There was no sign of people around, and the hole, which seemed to be a bottomless pit, had a tangle of rusty cables running down the sides and disappearing into the darkness. She backed cautiously away from the edge and then perked her ears up, listening.

"Lady!" Elbert Albert was calling from the campsite. "Come on, Lady!"

Lassie dropped her ears and hurried back, the smell of frying bacon now clearly discernable in the chilly air.

"Well!" Gus said with a smile when she arrived. "You been out doing some prospecting, Lady?"

Lassie nuzzled close to him and wagged her tail.

"This is famous mining country, did you know that Elbert Albert?" He poured a bowl of beaten eggs into the hot skillet and smiled at the surrounding countryside. "This is where the 'Unsinkable Molly Brown' got all her money. And Baby Doe Tabor, and a lot of others. A good part of the gold and silver came out of that gulch right over there."

Elbert Albert was in his sweatsuit doing exercises. "It's a beautiful place," he said. "Maybe that's what we ought to do, Gus, get ourselves a pick and shovel and get rich."

"I'm afraid we're a little late, Elbert Albert. About a hundred years."

After they ate Gus took the van into town for what he called some "horse trading," and Lassie followed Elbert Albert while he did some more running and shadow boxing. When Gus came back about noon he seemed pleased with things, and after lunch he advised Elbert Albert to take a good long nap. Lassie joined him, and altogether it was a pleasant afternoon. At about eight o'clock that night, she finally found out what was going on.

She didn't completely understand it at first. Gus got all dressed up in a suit and necktie, and Elbert Albert came out of the van wearing a white bathrobe. Then they all drove into town and around to the back of a building that said ODD FELLOWS HALL on the side.

From all the noise inside the place, it must have been packed with people. But Gus and Elbert Albert and Lassie went through a dark hall and into a tiny room that had a long table and a couple of hard chairs. There Elbert Albert lay down and they just waited, listening to the people shouting and whistling in the other part of the building. Finally a rough-looking man stuck his head in the door. "You're up," he muttered and disappeared.

"Okay," Gus said as they moved into the hallway. "Make it look good, Elbert Albert. Lots of pain and suffering. And this is a pretty tough audience. They like to see people slammed around, so give them plenty of body tosses."

Elbert Albert nodded, and they stopped at the door leading into the hall.

Except for the ring in the center, the place was dark and smoky and packed with people. In the ring a man wearing a bow-tie was reading from a small card. "The next event," he yelled out, "is a match featuring Mighty Manuel, the Masked Mauler from Mexico City . . ."

The man suddenly turned, and with his arm gesturing dramatically he pointed at the aisle directly across the room. There was a roar from the crowd and a huge man wearing purple trunks and a mask of black cloth came striding down the aisle.

Lassie had never seen anything like this, and it made her a little nervous. But Gus and Elbert Albert seemed unperturbed by the shouting and screaming.

"And his worthy opponent," the man with the bow-tie shouted, "Direct from Athens, Greece . . . known throughout the world as the Graceful Greek . . . the one and only . . . Apollo!"

Lassie had no idea what the man was saying. She looked around until she spotted Elbert Albert in back of the crowd, pulling on a wig of golden-yellow curls.

Lassie stared and then followed along as Elbert Albert gave her a wink and headed down the aisle with Gus. The people were screaming again; some of them reaching out to touch Elbert Albert as he strode by. Lassie stuck to Gus' heels and quickly jumped to the side as some of the hands grabbed at her.

Elbert Albert climbed up between the ropes and stood for a minute with his hands clasped over his head. The crowd roared, and Elbert Albert grinned and bowed. Then, as he slowly circled the ring, the man with the mask suddenly jumped from his little stool. As if crazed by some strange madness, he rushed across and slammed his elbow brutally into Elbert Albert's face.

Lassie reacted immediately. The crowd screamed, Elbert Albert staggered and fell to the canvas, and Lassie leaped toward the ropes, snarling, her teeth bared. But that was as far as she got. Gus suddenly had her by the collar and yanked her back to the floor.

"Easy, Lady, easy," he said. "It's all part of the act. Manuel's an old pal from Cincinnati."

"The best two out of three falls," the man with

the bow-tie shouted. "And may the best man win!"

Lassie moved to the corner with Gus and watched closely as a bell rang and the two men moved toward each other from the corners.

Miraculously, Elbert Albert seemed to have recovered completely from the blow. He came at the other man with his hands up, and the two of them circled each other for a minute. With his yellow curls dancing around his head, Elbert Albert suddenly grabbed at Manuel's head and missed. Then Manuel had Elbert Albert's foot, and with a sharp twist he dropped Elbert Albert to his back. Lassie growled, ready to jump again. Then she stared as Manuel turned quickly and threw himself into the ropes. Apparently it was his intention to come flying back and land on Elbert Albert. But Elbert Albert rolled away, and Manuel landed on the canvas with a painful thud. Lassie relaxed a little and then saw Gus smiling down at her. "You like that, do you?" he said.

Lassie barked, agreeing.

Elbert Albert finally landed a couple of blows to Manuel's face, and as the battle continued it seemed to Lassie that he was getting the best of it. They locked their arms around each other's heads, twisted each other's toes, locked legs into unnatural positions and slammed each other to the mat, all the while grimacing with pain and sometimes doubling over from hard blows to the stomach. Lassie growled a few times, but more often she eased back and panted, confident that the man named Manuel would soon give up the hopeless fight.

Then, to Lassie's surprise, Manuel suddenly seemed to have the upper hand. He locked his arm around Elbert Albert's head, and from the screams and the way his face was contorted, Elbert Albert was clearly in pain. Then he seemed to stand in a daze as Manuel suddenly released the grip, dropped his head and lifted Elbert Albert high in the air. Lassie blinked with disbelief as Manuel began spinning around with Elbert Albert still on his shoulders. Finally, with two quick steps, Manuel rushed to the side and Elbert Albert flew through the air and went sprawling into the empty aisle just behind Lassie and Gus. The crowd roared as if delighted by Elbert Albert's misfortune.

Lassie went quickly to his aid. Elbert Albert was moving slowly, dragging himself to his hands and knees, and Lassie licked frantically at his face. Then she turned abruptly and bounded toward the ring, her teeth bared and an angry snarl coming from her throat. Then she suddenly found herself suspended in mid-air, Gus holding her tightly with both arms.

"Hey, take it easy," he said. He pulled her away from the ropes and set her down, keeping a firm grip on her collar.

Lassie whimpered sympathetically as Elbert Albert struggled weakly to get back through the ropes. He looked terrible. His eyes were blurry, one arm was dangling uselessly at his side, and his legs seemed to wobble as he finally made it to the canvas and stumbled forward.

It was obvious that Elbert Albert was badly hurt and unable to defend himself. But everyone seemed to be screaming even louder, as if they wanted to see him dead.

Manuel looked like he was ready to accommodate them. With Elbert Albert standing in a daze in the middle of the ring, Manuel let out a gleeful cry and ran full speed toward the ropes again. Then, bouncing back as if he were a missile flying from a slingshot, he crashed into Elbert Albert, sending him sprawling once again on his face.

Elbert Albert was helpless now, but Manuel

came quickly to his feet again. With a running start, he bounded into the air and landed with his knees squarely in Elbert Albert's back.

Lassie had seen enough. With all her strength, she leaped upward, tearing herself from Gus' grip, then raced across the ring, snarling and barking. The two men were still down, and Lassie circled them, barking as loud as she could to get Manuel's attention.

The crowd was suddenly screaming twice as loud and then Lassie could hear laughter as the referee ran for the ropes and ducked out of the ring.

Elbert Albert was as surprised as everybody else to see Lassie circling around them. Manuel had a tight grip on his ears and was slamming his head into the canvas, and Lassie was coming closer and closer, snarling at Manuel as if ready to chew him up.

"Hey, Apollo," Manuel said, leaning close to his ear, "what's with your dog? Does she bite?"

Elbert Albert kept the pained look on his face as he answered. "Don't worry, she's a pussycat. She doesn't know how to bite."

As quickly as Elbert Albert spoke, Manuel screamed and shot to his feet, a look of pure panic on his face as he swung around. Behind him, her teeth clamped firmly into his purple trunks, was Lassie.

The whole place exploded now. Cushions and bottles were flying in the air; Manuel's trunks were tearing loose as he whirled Lassie around; Gus was dodging missiles and trying to climb into the ring; and everybody in the place was screaming hysterically and running for the doors, or into the ring.

"Lassie!" Gus screamed when he finally made it into the ring. He grabbed at Lassie, at the same time shouting at the wrestlers. "Elbert Albert, come on! The cops are coming! We've got to get out of here!"

Lassie still didn't let go of the purple trunks. But suddenly there was the sound of ripping and tearing! Just then, with Gus and Elbert Albert leading the way, Lassie bolted up the aisle and followed them through the dark corridor and out the back door.

10

After they escaped from the riot, Gus and Elbert Albert hurriedly packed, and then drove for two hours before Gus found a new camping place. But once they were bedded down, Lassie didn't sleep.

What disturbed her was Gus' comment about where they were going the next day. "We can have breakfast in Denver tomorrow morning," he'd said just before he climbed into his sleeping bag. "Then we can head south. Maybe stop in Colorado Springs for awhile."

"Colorado Springs sounds good to me," Elbert Albert answered sleepily.

Lassie had heard the words "Colorado Springs" many times. She associated them with Mr. Jamison and felt very uneasy when Gus mentioned them. Her hackles had risen when Gus said the words and her adrenalin was really flowing when Elbert Albert repeated them.

She waited until she was certain they were both sound asleep. Then, she carefully eased herself out from under Elbert Albert's arm. In the van there was an old bone she had been gnawing on for the past two days. She got it out and dropped it close to Elbert Albert's pillow. Next to Gus she placed the rubber ball he had bought for her in Leadville. Then she forced the green collar over her head and dropped it between them.

With a final backward glance at the two friends who had treated her so well, she trotted through the woods to the highway and headed west once again.

Gus thought he was having a nightmare at first. Sirens were blaring, tires were squealing and people were yelling at each other all around him. He turned over in his sleeping bag and after a minute lifted his head. Then he squinted, unable to see a thing beyond the blinding spotlight that was focused directly into his face.

"Okay, you guys, out of those bags," a gruff voice commanded. "Come on, fast!"

Gus still couldn't see anything. "What's going on? People are trying to sleep!"

"Police!" a man said. He came into view now, a man in a tan uniform. Behind him, other policemen were getting out of cars.

"We didn't call any police," Gus protested. He slid out of his bag, and Elbert Albert did the same.

"No," the man said, "we're doing the calling. Where's the dog?"

The dog? Had they come to arrest Lady for tearing Manuel's trunks? Gus looked at Elbert Albert, then they both glanced around. "She's gone!" Elbert Albert said.

"She was here when we went to sleep," Gus stammered.

The policemen stared suspiciously at them. "A couple hundred people saw the animal with you two guys at the wrestling match. We're here to pick her up. Get her!"

Gus blinked at the man, then rose and glanced around. "Lady," he called out. "Here, Lady!" He gave a shrill whistle through his teeth.

"Try the name *Lassie*," the policeman said.

Gus frowned, but gave it a try. "Lassie! Here, Lassie! Come on, girl!"

"Why do you want her?" Elbert Albert asked the man.

The man gave him a contemptuous look. "Put on your clothes; we're taking you in."

"On what charge?" Gus demanded.

"For stealing a large sable and white collie dog, last seen wearing a green leather collar. Answers to the name of Lassie."

Gus glanced quickly at Elbert Albert. "A green collar?"

"That's right," the policeman said. "Emerald green with brass studs."

Gus stared at the man, then looked down with surprise. The green collar was now lying beside his pillow. Next to it was the red rubber ball he had bought for Lady. He knelt and picked up the collar. "You mean like this?"

The policemen all stared at them, then stepped aside as a man dressed in a heavy camel's hair coat came out of the shadows. He took the collar from Gus and looked it over carefully.

"Yes, this is it, sheriff," he said, then looked at Gus. "Where did you find her?"

Gus had to think for a minute. "In Zion Canyon, two days ago. She was lame. Her right leg had some pulled ligaments and her foot was cut."

Jamison sighed and shook his head. "I'm not surprised her feet were banged up. As far as I know she walked all the way from Colorado Springs."

"Poor little Lady," Elbert Albert said.

"You have no idea where she is now?"

"No," Gus answered. "She was here when we went to sleep."

"When the cops woke us she was gone," Elbert Albert said. "Maybe those spotlights scared her."

"Then she couldn't be too far away," Jamison said. He looked thoughtfully at Gus and Elbert

Albert and the battered van standing behind them. Then he moved over to where a man in a chauffeur's uniform stood. "Here," he said, peeling off some bills from a fat roll of money. "Give 'em this."

The police moved back to the cars and the chauffeur brought the money to Gus.

"What's this for?" Gus asked.

The man in the camel's hair coat glanced at them from the shadows. "For board and veterinary service."

The chauffeur hurried back. Doors were slammed all around them, then gears were clashing and the army of cars began to retreat.

Gus stared at the disappearing cars and finally fanned out the wad of bills.

"Wow!" Elbert Albert said, "Five hundred big ones. I told you Lady had class."

"Yeah." Gus sighed. "Much as we need it, I'd rather have her than the money."

"You know, Gussie," Elbert Albert said, "I was just thinking . . ."

"Me too," Gus said.

"Why don't we get one of our own?"

"Right. There must be a pound around here somewhere."

Elbert Albert smiled. "An orphan. Lady would like that."

Gus grinned. "You bet she would." He tucked the bills into a pocket and crawled back into his sleeping bag. "Now, after we get the dog, we'll have the van worked on a little. And then we'll get you some new costumes to brighten up the act. Maybe a golden toga . . ."

"Wow, I'll be dazzling!" Elbert Albert said.

"Double-dazzling. And maybe we'll spend a little money on advance publicity. Our luck's turned, Elbert Albert. I can smell it!"

The telephone rang just after eight o'clock that night. Chris was in his bedroom putting on his pajamas, and he didn't pay much attention to it. But going across the hall to brush his teeth in the bathroom, he stopped for a minute, noticing the funny sound in his grandfather's voice.

"I don't understand, Mr. Jamison," Grandpa was saying into the phone. "Lassie is missing? You mean she ran away?"

Chris' heart stopped for a minute, and then it was racing at full speed as he moved closer to the top of the stairs.

"Of course I'll let you know if she shows up here, Mr. Jamison. But Colorado is a long way off. When did she run away?"

Chris was overjoyed for a minute. But just as quickly he pictured Lassie wandering all by herself through the Colorado mountains.

"You mean she's been gone for *five days!*" Grandpa exclaimed. "I see. Well, yes, we'll certainly keep an eye out for her. Thank you for calling, Mr. Jamison. Good-bye."

Chris' heart clamored in his chest as he waited for his grandfather to come upstairs and tell him the news. But then he heard Kelly and Grandpa talking softly in the kitchen. After ten minutes, it seemed clear that Grandpa was not coming up to tell him, and Chris finally went back to his room and sat thoughtfully on the bed.

Lassie had gotten away from the man! But where had she gone? Would she try to walk all the way from Colorado? Chris suddenly was frightened, picturing all the mountains and desert and dangerous highways between Glen Ellen and Colorado. How could she possibly make it by herself? She could starve to death, or get run over by a car, or even get lost somewhere in the wilderness. He had to find her. Somehow he had to find her and help her.

Chris worked it out carefully, and waited until morning before he put the plan into effect. At breakfast Grandpa said nothing to him about Lassie being missing. He and Kelly acted as if nothing had happened, and Chris said good-bye to them and got on the schoolbus as usual.

His heart was pounding, but he said nothing to his friends. When the bus reached the school he lagged back and was the last one to get off. Then, with the other kids off to their classrooms, he walked casually to the corner and crossed the street. When he was finally out of sight of the school building, he moved faster, heading off toward the highway. He would find her, he promised himself. If it took the rest of his life, he would search every foot of area between Glen Ellen and Colorado Springs.

"I'm coming, Lassie," he told her silently. God, he prayed, don't let anything happen to her before I get there.

Kelly didn't think much about it at first. She saw the schoolbus come swaying and groaning up the road, and she poured a glass of milk and got some cookies out for Chris. Then she heard the bus pass by without stopping and she peered out the window.

Had Chris said anything about staying after school? Or going to someone else's house? She couldn't recall his having mentioned it. She looked out the window and scanned the yard to be sure. Then she took off her apron and hurried out to the winery.

"Grandpa, the bus didn't stop."

"Huh?" Grandpa was measuring yeast mixtures into the barrels, and several other workers were labeling bottles.

"The bus didn't stop," Kelly repeated. "Chris didn't come home from school."

Grandpa frowned. "Is this Little League day?"

"He didn't say anything about it this morning." Kelly knew there might be a dozen good reasons for Chris not coming home on the bus, but for some reason it worried her. "I'm going to call the school, Grandpa."

"He's walked home before."

She moved to Grandpa's old desk and picked up the extension phone. "But he always told us first."

"Well, maybe this time he forgot."

She dialed and took a deep breath as she waited.

"Glen Ellen School," a cheery voice answered.

"Mr. Byington, this is Kelly Mitchell. Did Chris stay for Little League this afternoon?"

Mr. Byington seemed surprised by the question. "No, he didn't, Kelly. In fact Chris didn't come to school at all today, I assumed he was sick."

"He didn't come at all? Are you sure?"

"I'm quite sure. Is anything wrong?"

"I . . . I don't know, Mr. Byington. I'll let you know. Thank you."

Grandpa was staring hard at her when she hung up. "You mean to say he wasn't at school all day?!"

Kelly suddenly felt frightened. "No, Grandpa."

"Come on," he said and headed for the door. "Let's get into town."

Being sheriff in a quiet place like Glen Ellen, some people thought Frank Andrews had the easiest job in the world. It may have been true, but Frank worked hard at it, most of his efforts going toward keeping people from getting too excited about little problems. It had been his experience that most things worked themselves out with no interference from the law, and generally patience was both a healer and a problem-solver. Angry people cooled off and forgot trespassers and petty thefts, and people who were ready to break each other's noses on one day would generally be having coffee together the next.

When Clovis Mitchell and his granddaughter came storming into Frank's office with their story about Chris having disappeared, he listened silently until he heard all the facts.

"Well now, Clovis," he finally said, "I don't think I'd worry about it too much. Every kid plays truant now and then. Likely, two or three of them went fishing somewhere."

"Chris didn't play truant, Frank. And if he'd gone fishing he would have told us."

Frank sometimes wished he had counted the number of times kids had been reported missing by hysterical parents, and then showed up an hour later with a string of fish, or a bucketful of frogs. He shrugged and gave Clovis and Kelly an easy smile. "Well, there's a first time for everything. And now that school's started again, kids like to break away now and then." He rose and gave Kelly a wink. "Now why don't you both go on home. I'll bet he's waiting for you right now."

"Frank, are you refusing to help me?"

"Of course not." He glanced at his desk and all the paperwork he'd hoped to get finished today. "I'll tell you what—if Chris isn't home by midnight, you give us a ring, Clovis. I promise you, we'll get right to work on it."

Clovis stared at him for a minute, then wheeled and strode out the door.

"Grandpa, where are you going?" Kelly asked, following close behind.

They had brought the big car to town instead of the jeep. Clovis slid behind the wheel and hit the starter. "After him," he said. "You take care of things at home, and stay close to the phone. I'll call you later from somewhere in the general direction of Colorado."

"Colorado?"

Clovis probably didn't hear her as the car roared back and then sped off.

From across the street Allan Fogerty stared as the car swerved around two others and went careening toward the highway. When Kelly and Clovis had arrived in town, Allan had been the first person they'd told about Chris' disappearance.

"Where's he going?" Allan asked as he crossed the street.

"He said something about calling from Colorado."

Allan frowned and shook his head. "I've asked around at all the stores, but nobody remembers seeing him today."

"Thanks, Allan."

"You know, I'm worried about your grandfather —tearing off like that without knowing where he's going."

Kelly nodded thoughtfully. "Grandpa sometimes does things that don't seem to make sense at the time he does them. But there's always logic behind them."

"How can he possibly know where to look for Chris?"

Kelly shook her head, then smiled. "You know, I'll bet he finds him. Grandpa's wonderful in crises like this." She glanced from Allan to the empty space where the car had been parked. "I seem to be fresh out of transportation."

"I'll take you home."

While Allan drove, Kelly searched her mind trying to remember anything Chris might have said that would provide a clue to where he had gone. Last night when Mr. Jamison called, she and Grandpa had agreed it was best not to tell Chris about Lassie's having run away. It would only get his hopes up, and he would have to be disappointed again. Was it possible that Chris had overheard them talking? Or that he heard Grandpa talking to Mr. Jamison? She hoped not.

When they reached the house Allan got on the phone again and called all of Chris' friends. Kelly put some leftover casserole in the oven to warm and then went up to Chris' room.

She didn't see it at first. She looked in the closet to see what clothes were missing, and then under his pillow and on his desk, in case he might have left a note. Then her heart dropped as she stared at the piggy bank on the dresser. It was lying on its side. When she crossed the room and shook it, there was not a sound.

"Allan," she called and took it downstairs. "He's taken everything out of his bank."

Allan hung up the phone. "Well, if he took his money, he knew where he was heading. We'd better notify the sheriff and ask him to get an all-points bulletin out on Chris." He dialed and waited, but there was no answer. "Maybe he went out for a cup of coffee."

Kelly wondered how far Chris could get on the money he took from his bank. There couldn't have been much more than a few dollars in it. But it was the thought of his getting hurt, or lost somewhere, that worried her.

"This was always such a happy house," she said, suddenly feeling tears in her eyes. "It never had a chill before."

Allan reached across and took her hand. "They'll be all right. Don't lose faith in your grandpa."

"I haven't. It's just—so big and empty out there. And Chris is such a little boy. And Lassie isn't used to being alone."

"Kelly, if it's any consolation, that story Jamison gave your grandfather about a fire in the kennels? The fire department has no record of it."

Kelly looked at him, but her hopes quickly faded. "They probably put out the fire themselves."

"Yes, I'm sure that's what Jamison will say. But I intend to check out everyone who had anything to do with that litter of pups."

"You're very kind to us, Allan."

"I'm very fond of . . . of your family."

Kelly felt her face grow warm. She glanced at Allan, then picked up the phone. "Maybe I'd better call the sheriff again."

She dialed and held the receiver for two full minutes before she hung up. "There's still no answer."

Allan rose. "Well, it is Friday night and I guess he's busy. I'll go and look for him. You know where to reach me if you need me."

Kelly followed him out and he paused at the porch. "It's a beautiful night," he said.

"Allan . . . our family is very fond of you, too. And very grateful."

He smiled and Kelly edged back a little, wondering if she was being too forward with him. Then her heart sank as he turned and went down the steps. "Goodnight," he said.

"Goodnight," she whispered.

Somehow Kelly felt disappointed. Had she acted too aloof and cold with him? She watched him start the car and drive slowly toward the gate. Then she blinked as he suddenly put the car in reverse and started backing up.

He came all the way to the steps before he stopped. Then he was out of the door and up the steps in three long strides, and she was suddenly in his arms.

Kelly couldn't remember ever having been kissed so tenderly—or having it affect her quite so much. Then Allan drew back and smiled. "To be continued."

"Yes," she murmured.

This time he drove through the gate, and Kelly watched until his car finally disappeared over the crest of the hill. She walked slowly back into the house, not feeling quite so lonely now.

It was funny, she reflected as she returned to the kitchen. She had never pictured the kind of man she might fall in love with. Other girls seemed to be full of specifics about dark or light men with blond or brown hair, and at least a certain height. Some even had rigid requirements about the kind of car the man should own, and what his occupation had to be. For her, Allan seemed to far surpass any dreams she might have conjured. And now that she thought about it, she wasn't even sure what color his eyes were.

She took the casserole from the oven and suddenly realized that Allan hadn't eaten any dinner. She frowned, wondering where he would go and what he would eat. Then she felt guilty as she thought about the hundreds of times he must have sat in coffee shops and eaten dinner by himself. And breakfasts and lunches?

Kelly finally laughed at herself. Allan probably got along very well by himself. But after she turned out the lights and went to her bedroom, she looked out the window toward town, half wondering what he was doing at that precise minute.

11

Shortly after she left Gus and Elbert Albert and returned to the highway, Lassie saw the mass of flashing red lights racing toward her. As quickly as she scampered into the brush, the string of cars roared past and disappeared in the direction of the campsite. Half an hour later they went by again, going even faster as they headed toward Leadville.

When they were finally out of sight, Lassie resumed her westward trek, ducking into the woods or behind clumps of brush whenever the headlights of cars appeared. It was a dark, moonless night, and she had no idea what kind of ferocious animals might be lurking in those high mountains.

It was almost dawn when she came to the small roadside coffee shop. Five or six small cabins were scattered in the woods behind, but nobody seemed to be awake yet. Lassie nudged the lid off a big trash can at the rear of the restaurant, but there wasn't a scrap of food in it. She finally moved back to the edge of the forest and waited.

An hour passed before the sun rose above the mountain peaks to the east. Then an elderly couple came from one of the cabins and opened the back door of the coffee shop. They went inside, and several minutes later the man brought a big plastic bag out to the trash can. Lassie came instantly to her feet and trotted across the graveled parking area.

"Well! Where'd you come from, doggie?" the man said as he dropped the bag in the can. He knelt down and scratched her neck. "Haven't seen you around here before. You hungry?"

Lassie barked and licked his face.

"Well, I got something I'll bet you'll really like." He went back in the kitchen, talking all the while. "I was saving these for Mrs. Swanson's dog, but she's a little Pekinese about the size of your tail. I don't reckon she could handle more than one or two of them."

When he came back he was unwrapping six T-bones from a piece of newspaper. "Some of these still got a good bit of meat on 'em. With the price of steaks these days, it's amazing what some people leave on their plates." He flattened the paper out as if spreading a napkin for Lassie. "Blanche, come on out here and look at this pretty collie dog!"

"We got customers, Nate."

Lassie gave the man a thank-you bark as he closed the door. Then she gathered up as many of the bones as she could carry and took them to the bushes.

The coffee shop appeared to be a popular place. Within the next twenty minutes three pick-up trucks and a camper pulled in. Then a big oil tanker parked near the road and the driver left his motor running as he went inside.

Lassie considered the possibilities as she gnawed on the bones. The camper and one of the pick-up trucks had come in from the east, so presumably they would continue west when the drivers finished eating. On the other hand, they could belong to people who lived in the area. She couldn't be sure, and she didn't want to risk being taken the wrong way again. Then her head suddenly lifted and she perked her ears up.

A big white car with a boat trailing behind it was turning into the parking lot. In the back seat of the car two children were peering out the window at the coffee shop. What caught Lassie's attention were the license plates on both the car and the boat-trailer. They struck a familiar chord. Somehow they reminded Lassie of the plates on Allan Fogerty's car.

Lassie immediately picked up two of the T-bones in her teeth and trotted quickly across the parking area. With a single jump she bounded from the fender of the trailer to the inside of the boat.

The worst part for Chris was the blasting wind and the smell of diesel smoke as it whipped past. He was no longer afraid of falling off the big truck. Once he had climbed to the top of the canvas-covered load he had snaked his arm around the tie-ropes and braced his feet against a ridge in the uneven surface. But through the afternoon, the heat and wind and sooty smoke had battered unmercifully at him. The big truck rattled and vibrated, and all around him the canvas fluttered and popped, and Chris kept his head under his arm as much as he could.

After he left the school that morning, he had avoided the town as much as possible. He had skirted around where there were only a few scattered houses, and nobody seemed to notice him. Then he had walked south for two or three miles before a man in an old car pulled over and picked him up. "I missed the schoolbus," Chris told the man, to explain his presence on the road. The man had let him off in the next town, and from there he had hitchhiked to Vallejo. The second driver was about eighty years old and didn't seem to have any curiosity about a ten-year-old boy hitchhiking.

The big truck was parked by a restaurant when Chris spotted it. The motor was running and it was pointed east, and when nobody was looking he climbed up the side and flattened himself so he couldn't be seen from below. Five minutes later he heard the door of the cab slam shut. Then the motor was roaring and sputtering as the driver shifted gears and they pulled onto the road and began to gather speed. With all the jiggling and vibration, Chris quickly secured himself more firmly in the ropes, and with one hand he managed to open his lunchbox and eat a sandwich. Then the lunchbox was suddenly caught in the wind and swept away.

It was blistering hot through most of the afternoon. Then, as the sun went down and they climbed high into the mountains, Chris found himself shivering. Finally they seemed to have reached the summit, and the truck sputtered and backfired as they weaved and swayed down a long, winding highway.

Chris was numbed with weariness as he clung to the ropes. He curled himself up as tight as he could and thought about Lassie through most of the trip. Wherever she was, she must be cold and hungry. And there must be all kinds of wild animals in the Colorado mountains. She wouldn't know where to go, or how to find anything to eat, and with all his money Mr. Jamison probably had every police department in the state looking for her.

He had to find her, Chris told himself. He had to let her know that he still loved her, and that neither he nor Kelly nor Grandpa had abandoned her. That was the worst part of it—the fear that Lassie might think they had all forgotten her.

The truck seemed to have reached the bottom

of the mountains, and it was warm again as they roared along a broad freeway. Chris finally lifted his head and stared at the mass of bright lights off to the side. They were passing a large city with tall buildings and an unusual number of flashing signs. But the driver kept going at full speed.

For a minute Chris wondered if there were two drivers in the cab, and if they might keep traveling all night and pass right through Colorado. But then he remembered his geography and the fact that Colorado was on the other side of Nevada and Utah. Somewhere in-between they would have to stop for fuel.

Five minutes later his fears were eased. The roar of the motor suddenly softened and they slowly lost speed. Then, a moment before they pulled off the highway, Chris glimpsed the sign on the other side of the road. *Sacramento 123 mi., Reno 8 mi.*, it said.

The city they had passed must have been Reno, Nevada.

A minute later the truck was slowly weaving its way through a mass of other trucks. Then the air-brakes let out a loud hiss and they stopped.

Chris had never seen so many diesel trucks parked in one place—most of them with their motors still running. On his own truck, the driver switched off the headlights, and a moment later the door slammed and Chris saw the man walking off toward a broad, rambling building in the midst of the trucks. A big neon sign across the top of the building said BOOMTOWN—RESTAURANT/ENTERTAINMENT.

His arm was so stiff he could hardly move it once he had extracted himself from the ropes. His legs were also numb, and he lowered himself slowly and carefully down the side of the truck.

The din of rattling diesel motors was deafening as he made his way past the trucks. When he reached the glass door of the building, he paused for a minute, watching the mass of people inside. The place was mobbed, most of the people clustered around long tables where they were shouting and laughing. He finally pushed the door open, and once again his ears were assaulted by a crash of noise.

From one side of the huge room came the clatter and crash of game machines. In the center, the players were yelping and shouting, and from the other side a group of musicians sounded as if they were trying to drown out all the other noises. Farther back in the room were games with flashing lights and spinning wheels and little Ping-Pong balls bouncing in cages.

Chris moved wearily through the room, fascinated, but a little frightened by all the noise and activity. Nobody seemed to notice him as he passed the card game tables and moved to the left along the rear wall. Then he stopped and gazed at a small sign above an open door. KIDDIELAND, it said. He moved forward and peered inside.

Chris had never been to Disneyland, but he imagined a good part of it looked like this. The track of a miniature roller-coaster circled the entire perimeter of the room. To his right was an oval track with child-size racing cars, and farther along were several dozen pinball machines and a place with targets and electronic rifles.

Chris stared numbly at everything, too tired to appreciate the wonder of it all. He finally edged inside and touched the steering wheel of one of the race cars. Then he moved on, trailing his fingers along the machine's polished hood.

From the race cars he crossed to a jet airplane that was perched on a high swivel. He climbed the two steps and seated himself in the

cockpit, dazzled by the array of dials and gauges.
With his head resting on the soft leather cushion,
he gazed at the switch that said *Power On*. As
he reached for it he closed his eyes for a second.
Then his shoulders sagged, his head settled com-
fortably on the instrument panel and he was fast
asleep.

With the desert winds blasting through the
open window of the car and the lights of Reno
brightening the skyline ahead, Clovis Mitchell
once again speculated on Chris' probable be-
havior.

Earlier, he had decided it was highly doubtful
Chris could have hitchhiked any significant distance from Glen Ellen. He might have made it a
few miles, but if he tried to thumb a ride on a
major highway, nine people out of ten would
have been suspicious and reported it to the police. Chris probably knew that, or found it out
very quickly, and he would have figured his best
chance was to hide inside a truck going east.
And, as no phone calls had come from the police
during the day, he must have been successful at
it.

Clovis had inquired at every big truck stop between Vallejo and Reno, but nobody had seen any
sign of him. The question in Clovis' mind now
was: was it worth it to stop in Reno and ask
around? Would Chris be likely to get off a truck
in a big city like that? Or would he keep moving
and try to cover as much distance as possible?

With each decision Clovis knew he was overlooking some possibilities. But searching by himself, he had to stick with only the most probable
answers. As he whipped past the off-ramps dropping into Reno, he prayed once again that he
was doing the right thing. At the other stops
they had told him there was a big truck terminal

six or eight miles east of Reno, and that seemed like his best bet right now.

There was no mistaking the location of the terminal. Parked around the building with the big sign flashing BOOMTOWN, it looked like there were two or three hundred diesel trucks. After he parked, Clovis spent an hour in the casino and restaurant questioning anybody who looked even remotely like a truck driver. Then he trudged over to the motel office and rented a room.

He was discouraged, but still determined, and he would not permit himself to think about all the terrible things that could have happened to Chris. In spite of his actions in leaving home, the boy was level-headed and careful. Clovis pulled off his jacket and shoes and stretched out on the bed with his arm across his eyes. He should phone Kelly, he told himself. Kelly would have called Frank Andrews by now, and maybe they had heard something. Clovis reached across and put his hand on the telephone, but he was too tired to lift it. He took a long, weary breath and within two seconds he was asleep.

Motorcycle-officer Thomas Muldoon had signed his name on the duty roster. He had looked over the reports filed by the officers on the night shift, and he had glanced at the lists of hot cars and "wanted" criminals, and various other notices on the bulletin board. Then he finished his coffee and went out to where his motorcycle was parked in front of the Highway Patrol station.

It was too early in the morning for much traffic out there in the desert. A diesel tanker lumbered past with a little Volkswagen following behind—both of them cautiously making a complete stop at the highway intersection. Muldoon straddled his cycle and pulled on his gloves, then glanced over at the big white car coming to a

stop at the same intersection. The car was
headed west—a beautiful cabin cruiser resting
on the trailer behind it. Muldoon gazed envious-
ly at the boat as the car crossed the intersection
and started picking up speed. Then he blinked
and stared hard at the rear of the boat.

For a minute he wondered if his eyes were
playing tricks on him. Two minutes ago he had
been staring at a poster with a picture of a collie
dog on it. Now, with its ears perked up and its
mouth partially open, that same collie dog was
staring at him from the back of that boat. Muldoon quickly switched on the ignition and kicked
his motorcycle to life.

How much was the reward on that poster? A
thousand dollars? Two thousand? He roared onto
the highway and gave his bike full throttle, at
the same time switching on his red lights and
siren.

He was doing seventy and rapidly closing the
gap when the stoplights came on at the back of
the car and the driver edged toward the shoulder
of the road. He switched off the siren and ap-
plied the brakes, easing the bike to a stop just in
front of the car.

"I wasn't exceeding the speed limit, officer,"
the driver protested as Muldoon swung off the
bike and walked to the side of the car.

"No one said you were." Muldoon nodded toward the trailer. "You own that collie back there
in the boat?"

"Collie? In the boat?" The man stared at him,
and the two children in the back seat twisted to
look out the window. "We've got a German
shepherd, but he's at home."

Muldoon nodded. "That may be, sir, but I have
reason to believe you have a missing collie named
Lassie in your boat."

The man quickly opened the door and they both walked back. Muldoon expected to find the animal at the rear of the boat where he had last seen her. But suddenly the dog was looming over him, her front paws on the edge of the deck.

"Well, I'll be . . ." the man exclaimed.

Muldoon quickly turned and grabbed for Lassie's front legs. Then he let out a cry and stumbled backward as Lassie went flying over his head.

"Grab her!" he shouted—but he knew it was too late.

Lassie skidded for a moment in the middle of the highway, then she was racing past the car and down the shoulder at full speed. Muldoon scrambled to his feet and ran for the motorcycle.

"Go, Lassie, go!" the two kids shouted as Muldoon kicked the motor into action and roared away.

The dog was smart, Muldoon decided. As quickly as he drew within a hundred feet of her she made a sharp turn and crossed the highway. Then she dropped into the culvert at the side of the road and leaped over a barbed-wire fence.

Muldoon hesitated only long enough to check his rear-view mirror. Then he gave the cycle full throttle and went sailing over the fence behind her. When he landed he fishtailed for a moment, then gave it full throttle again. The dog was smart, but Thomas Muldoon had won a dozen trophies in motorcross races. He was the Evel Knievel of the Utah State Highway Patrol.

Again the dog made a sharp turn, this time racing up a slope and leaping across a twenty-foot gorge. Muldoon smiled to himself and gunned the cycle up the hill—sailing across the gorge as smoothly as a gazelle.

Things were a little tougher on the other side

of the gorge. The terrain was strewn with heavy boulders, and the dog could make quicker turns than he could. But the motorcycle was faster.

Muldoon saw her tail disappear around a big rock fifty yards ahead of him and he roared at full speed through the sand and dust to cut her off. When he reached the far side of the rock he spun through a half turn and skidded to a halt, ready to jump off and grab her.

He couldn't believe it for a minute. The dog was not there. Nor was she anywhere to the left or right. He turned sharply in his seat and then stared. Fifty yards behind him the dog was sitting on a big boulder, calmly watching him. He gunned the bike through a sharp turn and raced at full speed across the rocky terrain again.

Again he came to a screeching halt, and again the dog was nowhere in sight. A minute later, from the direction of the gorge, he heard a loud bark. The dog was standing in the open now, as if challenging him to catch her.

Muldoon had had enough. Without taking his eyes from Lassie, he twisted the throttle, roared through a fast turn and took off directly at her.

Lassie edged to the side as the machine went screaming across the sand. Then, at the last instant, she leaped over a high mound of boulders.

His jaw clenched tight and his eyes narrowed almost shut, Muldoon kept his gaze fixed only on the dog. When she edged to the side he quickly adjusted his course. Then, at the last minute when Lassie jumped, he swung the bike sharply to the left, expecting to run her down the moment she landed.

Instead of the dog, Muldoon saw only a feathery tail disappear behind a pile of rocks—and it was too late to turn. In the next instant the seat of the motorcycle leaped up beneath him. Then the bike was gone and he was sailing through the air, flailing frantically, trying to slow his rapid descent.

In the entire gully, with its tiny trickle of water, there was only one stagnant pool. Muldoon glimpsed the shiny surface for a fraction of a second, and then he slammed headlong into it, sending a spray of mud and water splattering against the far embankment.

For a minute Lassie thought the officer might be dead. Then, very slowly his arms drew in and he raised himself to his hands and knees. Glaring furiously at her, he scraped a handful of mud from his face and finally rose.

"I'll kill her!" he shouted and shook a muddy fist in the air. "I'll kill her!"

Lassie gazed silently at him for a minute, then trotted back to the highway.

The man and woman and the two children were all standing at the edge of the highway. The man smiled as Lassie trotted past. "Well, kids," he said, "after what we've just seen, I'll buy everyone a mile-high fudge sundae."

The kids cheered as they headed back to the car.

Lassie didn't follow them. She crossed the road and trotted off toward a railroad track she had noticed a couple hundred yards to the north. She didn't think it would be wise to travel any farther with those people.

12

Chris awakened slowly. Children were laughing and shouting and strange noises surrounded him; rumbling trains, dinging pinball machines, sharp reports from rifles being fired. For a moment he was uncertain where he was. Then he lifted his head and blinked into the face of a five-year-old girl with long blonde curls.

"Why are you sleeping in there?" the girl asked.

The whole place still seemed unreal. He frowned at the instrument panel and the control stick between his legs. Then he watched the girl's hand reach into the cockpit and press the power button.

Chris quickly grabbed the sides of the cockpit as the plane roared and vibrated and suddenly tilted forward as if in a sharp dive. "Hey, wait a minute! Hold still a minute!"

The girl giggled and punched the button again, stopping all the noise and movement. "This is the best ride in the room," she said. "Can I play on it for a while?"

Chris looked off at the thirty or forty kids in the room, then closed his eyes through a yawn. "Sure," he said and climbed out.

"You get some shut-eye," the little girl said

and took his place. "I'll take the mail on in to Los Angeles."

Chris nodded and moved away, still not quite awake. There weren't as many people in the room as the night before. Chris moved around the side of the room again until he reached the glass doors leading into the restaurant. The sight of so many people eating suddenly brought a deep ache to his stomach, and he pushed through the door. He moved uncertainly toward the cash register where a man wearing a leather jacket was paying his bill.

"So long, Ella," the man said when he got his change. "See you next week."

The woman smiled and stuck a pencil in her hair. "Have a good trip, Ed. Watch out for Smokey."

"You bet."

"Mister?" Chris blurted out almost before he realized he was speaking, "are you going to Denver?"

The man gave him a friendly smile. "I'm afraid not, sonny. I'm headed for Seattle, Washington. Sorry."

Chris nodded. "Thanks anyhow."

The waitress named Ella gave him a strange look as he moved to the counter. She was a heavy woman with a pleasant, motherly face.

"Hi there! What can I do for you?" she asked as she cleared away dirty dishes.

Chris looked at the menu items listed on the wall behind her. "Can I get anything for fifty cents?"

"Sure. Is that all you've got?"

"No, ma'am. But I've got a long way to go."

She quickly set out a napkin and silver. "Well, you're in luck. We just happen to have a special on today. How do you like your eggs?"

"Sunny side up."

"You've got it. Do you live in Denver?"

"No."

She looked curiously at him, then smiled and filled a glass with orange juice. From the refrigerator she brought out two eggs and a slice of ham, then dropped two pieces of bread into the toaster. "You got relatives there?" she asked.

"No," he said. "I'm going to see someone about something."

"You're kind of young to be on your own, aren't you?"

"Well . . . I'm small for my age, they tell me." He quickly looked off at the other customers, and she turned back to the grill. When she finally brought the big plate of food she watched him eat for a minute.

"Problems, huh?" she said quietly.

Chris didn't know what to say. He kept his eyes down and ate as fast as he could.

"Want to tell me about them?" Ella asked. "I'm a real good listener."

Chris tried to give her an unconcerned smile. "Thanks anyway."

"Hey, Charlie!" she suddenly yelled across the room. "Punch number thirty-seven on that juke box for me, will ya?"

"Sure thing, Ella."

She smiled and gave Chris a wink. "When I'm down in the dumps, this one always picks me up."

The song was about life being made of smiles and frowns, with lots of ups and downs.

Ella moved off and brought back a stack of hotcakes for him. "All that gloomy, all that glee," she said, echoing the words of the song. "Honey or syrup with your hotcakes?"

"Syrup, please," Chris said. He was feeling better now—unsure if it was from the food or the song. He pushed aside the emptied plate and dug into the hotcakes.

"A long time since dinner, huh?" Ella asked.

Chris smiled. "Yes, ma'am. You cook almost as good as my sister does."

She laughed. "Thanks. Where does your sister live?"

"In Glen Ellen, California."

Ella filled his milk glass and moved away. When she came back she was stuffing two huge sandwiches into a brown bag. "Your sister know you're here?" she asked.

The question seemed casual enough, but Chris suddenly felt a little alarmed. He wiped his face with the napkin and slid off the stool. "No . . . Well, I'd better be getting along."

She followed him to the cash register, and Chris put fifty cents on the counter. "What about tax?" he asked as she rang it up.

"Tax is included." She smiled and handed him the brown bag. "And this is on the house."

"Gee, thanks . . . Ella."

"Take care of yourself, honey," she said as he went out.

It was already hot and windy, and Chris paused for a minute outside the door. The steady roar of the trucks was now even louder than the night before. Like huge mechanical dinosaurs, they were hissing and belching and coughing out clouds of black diesel smoke. Chris moved hesitantly across the gravel apron to the first of the trucks. It had three license plates—California, Nevada and Arizona. He walked along its length and crossed in front of several others. Some of the license plates were so dirty he couldn't read them. But he didn't see any from Colorado.

He passed behind another truck and then quickly jumped back as a huge cab slid past within inches of him. The driver yelled down from his window, but Chris couldn't make out what he said. Five sets of giant tires crunched past, and then Chris hurried to cross the open gap.

For a moment he froze, transfixed by the sudden appearance of two trucks coming at him from the other direction. Should he go left or right? One of the trucks was picking up speed, and for an instant Chris stared at the Colorado license plate just below the bumper. Then the headlights came on and the truck's air horn sounded an urgent blast.

Chris' heart leaped into his throat when he looked up from the license plate and realized the truck was almost on top of him. Turning to run, his feet suddenly were gone from beneath him and he was sprawled face-down on the gravel. An instant later the sun was blotted out; he was surrounded by wheels and the hissing and screeching of brakes. Then the greasy oil-pan of a rattling engine was stopped three inches above his head.

"My God!" he heard the driver shout as the door slammed and the man's feet suddenly appeared at the side.

Chris grabbed the bag of sandwiches that had fallen from his hand and wriggled out in the other direction. He came instantly to his feet and ran, paying no attention to the swirl of moving wheels and looming radiators. Suddenly it seemed as if every truck in the parking lot was trying to run him down.

"Hey, kid!" the man behind him yelled.

Horns blasted, brakes hissed and squealed, and Chris ran faster, dodging one way and then the other, his heart pounding in his throat.

Other drivers were getting out of their trucks and yelling at him, and Chris ducked under a parked trailer. On the other side an empty cattle truck was standing a few feet away. Without hesitating, he pulled himself up to the level of the bed and scrambled up the wooden slats to the top. He stopped for a moment, undecided whether or not to go down the other side; then the decision was made for him. The big exhaust pipe rising next to the cab suddenly let out a throaty roar and the truck started moving.

Chris flattened himself on the jiggling boards, clinging tightly to a cross brace. Behind him he could see three or four drivers shouting after them as the truck gathered speed and turned on-to the highway. Then he looked quickly around and breathed a sigh of relief. They were headed east.

He closed his eyes and lay still for several minutes, catching his breath. Then he reached down as far as he could and dropped the bag of sandwiches into the dirty straw below. Then, cautiously keeping a tight grip on the jiggling cross brace, he eased through the boards and dangled for a minute. When he dropped to the truck bed it was bouncing and swaying so heavily he was unable to keep his feet. He was thrown to one side and then the other, and several minutes passed before he was able to anchor himself against one of the sideboards.

"I'd like to place a long-distance call, operator. To Glen Ellen, California."

Clovis blinked sleepily and shook his head in an effort to get the last of the grogginess out. He gave the number to the operator and Kelly answered after the first ring.

"Grandpa? Are you all right? Where are you?"

"I'm all right. I'm in a place called Boomtown. That's Boom, as in ta-ra-ra-boom-di-ay. Never mind the jokes. Have you got any news?"

"No, except Sheriff Andrews got that all-points

bulletin out. I'm checking the wine temperatures right now. Everything's under control."

"Okay, honey. I haven't found any trace of Chris yet, but you stay right there in case I call."

"I'll be here, Grandpa. And please take care of yourself."

After he hung up, Clovis went to the office and paid his bill. "What's all the commotion out there?" he asked the man. Truck drivers were yelling and blasting their horns at each other as if there were some kind of war going on.

The man chuckled. "There's so many trucks comin' in and out of here and they get all snarled up in a traffic jam sometimes."

Clovis considered going into the restaurant for some breakfast, but it looked as crowded as the parking lot. Instead he went directly to his car and headed east again.

In the restaurant, Ella gaped in surprise as a dozen truck drivers came pouring through the door. "You guys having a union meeting or something?"

The driver in the lead shook his head. "Some kid really tangled things up out there. I nearly killed him. He was staring at the license plates and I didn't even see him for a minute."

"A little fellow with light brown hair and a yellow shirt?"

"He was little, all right. A little . . ."

"Harry—watch your language in here. I don't allow it." She put a cup of coffee in front of him. "That kid was trying to get to Denver."

"Oh yeah? Well, if that was him, he jumped a cattle truck going to Keddie."

"Hey, quiet a minute," one of the other drivers said. He was squinting at the television set behind the counter.

It was a news bulletin of some kind; the announcer reading from a sheet of paper. "The F.B.I. has now been called into the search for young Christopher Mitchell," the man said. "Missing from his home in Glen Ellen, California, since yesterday morning, the boy . . ."

"Glen Ellen!" Ella shrieked. "That's where he's from!"

"Grandson of Clovis Mitchell," the announcer went on, "owner of the Mitchell Winery, Christopher was last seen by his classmates on the schoolbus yesterday morning."

A picture of Chris suddenly appeared on the screen.

"It's him!" Ella cried. "What did they say his grandfather's name was?"

"Clovis Mitchell," one of the drivers said.

"Light brown hair," the announcer went on, "blue-eyed, ten years old, four-feet-two-inches tall, weighing about seventy pounds."

Ella quickly found a dime in her pocket and moved out from behind the counter. "Harry, handle the register for me. I'm going to make a phone call."

After driving for an hour and a half, Clovis wished he had gotten something to eat at the Boomtown restaurant. Since leaving the motel he'd seen nothing but rocks and sand and sagebrush, and ahead of him it looked like another hundred miles of empty desert.

Until the last minute, Clovis didn't notice the car coming up fast behind him. It loomed in his rear-view mirror for a moment and then it swerved out and held a position directly beside him. It was a police car, and the man on the passenger side suddenly opened the window and stuck out a bullhorn.

"Gray Buick sedan," the harsh voice said, "California license number JLY 919, kindly pull over to your right."

The needle of his speedometer was hovering exactly on fifty-five. Clovis glanced at the man and gently eased off to the shoulder of the road. "Confounded police," he muttered to himself, "why aren't they out chasing criminals?"

The police car stopped behind him and Clovis rolled down the window. He had no intention of getting out. A moment later a young black man appeared at the side of the car.

"I was *not* speeding," Clovis said emphatically.

"You certainly weren't, Mr. Mitchell," the man said politely.

"Then what am I being accused of?"

"Sheriff Andrews in Glen Ellen asked us to flag you down, sir. And to give you all possible assistance. We have news of your grandson."

Clovis felt his heart suddenly stop beating. "Is he . . . is he all right?"

"As far as we know, he is. Please lock your car and come with us."

At times the freight train rolled along very slowly—creaking and rumbling at a pace no faster than a person could walk. Then it would gather speed and roar along with the cars rocking and clattering as if ready to fly off the tracks at any moment.

In the empty freight car Lassie lay by the half opened door watching mile after mile of hot Nevada desert pass by. When she first saw the train coming along the tracks behind her, she had moved to the side and watched it pass, thinking there was no possibility of boarding it. But then it had slowed to a crawl, and she had trotted alongside looking at each of the cars until she spotted the open door. With one leap she had easily jumped inside.

Well hidden from the view of helicopters or police cars, she had slept for awhile. Then she had gazed out at the endless miles of desert, wondering how far west the train might take her.

Now there seemed to be a few trees and green bushes along the way, and she could see a highway paralleling the track several hundred yards away. Then she heard the steady dingling of a railroad-crossing signal somewhere ahead.

An empty cattle truck was stopped on the highway, waiting for the train to pass. Lassie gazed indifferently at the truck and then blinked curiously as she saw what looked like a small arm hooked around one of the wooden slats in the rear of the truck. It looked as if a small child—maybe the driver's son—was riding in the back of the truck, hanging tightly to the board to keep from being bounced around. Then the truck was gone from sight, and she sighed heavily and gazed out at the desert again.

They were moving more slowly now, and ten minutes later Lassie heard the dinging bell of another crossing. She glanced ahead, then quickly backed away from the door into the shadows.

This time a police car was waiting, its red lights flashing as the two officers in the front seat gazed resignedly at the passing train. Lassie kept well out of sight until the tinging bell was far behind.

"That's the longest freight train I've ever seen," Clovis said from the back seat of the police car.

"It's pretty long, all right," the black officer agreed.

Clovis sighed and watched impatiently for the end of the train. "Just how did you fellas put this all together?" he asked.

"A lady saw your youngster in a restaurant," the black officer said. "She called your home in Glen Ellen and someone at your house called your local sheriff with your license number and a description of your car."

Clovis nodded, remembering the reception he had gotten from Sheriff Andrews yesterday. "Remarkable what you fellows can do when you set your minds to it."

"One of the truckers saw your grandson hop on an empty cattle truck," the other officer said. "We figure the truck is headed for a place called Keddie Wye, a few miles west of here. It's a big cattle-shipping terminal."

The caboose finally came into view. "There's the end," Clovis said. "Let's not let any grass grow under our feet."

The black man laughed and put the car in gear. "Right on, Mr. Mitchell."

The moment the caboose passed, the man switched on the siren and roared across the tracks.

Fifteen minutes later when the train came to a stop, Lassie didn't know what to think. Ahead of them the tracks forked into two sets, one of them curving off to the north. From inside the freight car she watched as several railroad men with lunchpails walked over to the train and climbed aboard. Others spoke to them for a minute and then got off the train and headed toward a small building. It looked as if the crew was being changed, and Lassie had an uneasy feeling that the train would take the right fork and head north when it started up again.

She moved cautiously to the edge of the car

and jumped down, quickly hiding behind the wheels. Fifty feet away, a pine-covered embankment rose above the level of the train. Lassie watched until none of the crew was looking in her direction, then inched out from under the freight car and trotted directly toward the slope.

No one called out or shouted an alarm, and a minute later she was scampering through the pine trees and over the small hill.

On the far side the highway curved around the base of the hill. Lassie moved down close to it and then dropped low, half hiding herself when she reached the culvert running alongside.

In the distance a siren was wailing, and a moment later a police car roared through the curve just above her head. When it was gone she scrambled out of the culvert and sniffed the air for a minute. Then she headed west again.

Chris' entire body was numb from the swaying and bouncing of the truck bed. He held tightly to the wooden slat and rested his head on his arm, but with every bump he was tossed several inches in the air and slammed down again. Finally, ten minutes after they had stopped to let the train go by, the truck rolled slowly to a stop. A moment later he heard the door of the cab slam shut as the driver got out.

They were in a cattle yard of some kind. Chris could hear bellowing, and the voices of cowboys yelling at the animals. He eased his bruised arm away from the wooden slat and started to get up. Then he ducked as he saw the driver suddenly reappear and climb into the cab.

The big diesel engine roared and they moved forward about fifty feet. Then the gears clashed and a moment later the truck was being backed up. Chris looked behind him and saw that they were angling steadily toward a high platform that had wooden fences at the sides. Just before they reached it, someone swung open the rear gates of the truck.

Chris stared and then felt his heart jump as the heads of several steers appeared, moving up a ramp and into the truck.

"Come on, get goin' there!" a voice cried out from somewhere behind the cattle. "Colby, give that big black a kick!"

The first three or four steers moved hesitantly into the truck, their glassy eyes staring wildly and their horned heads swinging from side to side. They moved a few feet and stopped, as if terrorized by their new surroundings. Then they bellowed and stumbled forward as the cowboys yelled and cursed behind them.

Chris screamed for help as the big animals edged closer and closer. With his back against the wooden slats, he swung the bag of sandwiches back and forth in front of the animals. But they came steadily forward, pushed by the crowd of cattle behind.

Chris screamed again, but the bellowing and the pounding of hooves on the truck bed drowned out his cries. The first animal was within five feet of him now, and he rushed to the side and squeezed his face into the gap between the slats, screaming once again.

Off to the side he saw the flashing red lights, and over the bellowing and thumping of hooves he heard the siren. Then a police car skidded to a stop fifty feet from the truck.

"Grandpa!" he screamed when the car doors flew open and he saw Clovis. "Grandpa!"

A black policeman was running toward the truck, at the same time waving at someone at the rear. "Get those animals back!" he shouted. "There's a child in there!"

Chris was suddenly knocked from his feet as a big steer turned and swung his haunches around. On the floor he could see only legs and hooves, all of them moving as the animals shifted in the tight quarters. He ducked under one of the steers and squeezed into the narrow space between the animal and the side of the truck. "Grandpa!" he screamed again.

"Grab my arm!" a voice cried out from somewhere above him.

Chris looked up and saw the black police officer hanging from the cross brace, his arm extended. He grabbed the man's forearm and felt a powerful grip on his own arm just below the shoulder.

"Hang on!" the man shouted. Then Chris was being lifted from his feet and hoisted upward.

"Get your foot on that crossboard!" the man said.

Chris kicked out with both feet until he found the board. Then the officer shifted and Chris went upward again, this time all the way to the top. Straddling the boards, the officer gently eased him down into Grandpa's arms.

"Chris! Thank Heavens you're safe!" Grandpa said as they hugged each other. "Thank Heavens you're safe!"

After she left the train that afternoon, Lassie traveled westward for another twenty miles. At dusk she came to a river and followed it downstream a few hundred yards to a waterfall. Several deer looked up and continued drinking as she made her way down to the pond below. After she had satisfied her thirst, she limped into the nearby brush and fell into an exhausted sleep. She was satisfied with her progress for the day. After her ride in the boat, and then the encounter with the motorcycle policeman, she had traveled a considerable distance on the freight train. If she could do as well tomorrow, she would be home in four or five days.

At dawn the soft patter of rain awakened her. She moved down to the pond and drank once more, than trotted back toward the highway as a clap of thunder was followed by a sudden drenching downpour.

13

The torrential battering of rain seemed like it would never end. It drummed ceaselessly on the roof of the winery; it battered the grapevines into sagging clumps, and it overflowed the culverts and irrigation ditches, and turned the dirt road into a muddy quagmire.

From the door of the winery, Clovis gazed dejectedly at the soggy fields and the gloom of gray hovering over them, and wondered how long it would go on. Another twelve hours of it would deal a serious blow to the vineyard. Vines would be uprooted, and a good portion of the topsoil could be washed away. On top of all their other troubles they didn't need that.

He looked over at the house for a minute before he returned to his work. Chris was still there—still standing silently at his bedroom window, watching the hills to the east. The boy still had hopes that sooner or later Lassie would appear on one of those hills, and come running down to the house.

Clovis was not so optimistic. He had no doubts that Lassie would try to come home. But the distance between Colorado and California was a lot of ground to cover. And any one of a hundred things could have happened to her. Jamison, with all his helicopters and reward money, and all his influence with the police, had been unable to find her. Lassie could have been picked up by somebody traveling east, or she might have found a good home in Colorado or Utah, or any one of a dozen other states. In any case, if she were found, she would have to be returned to Jamison, and Clovis was convinced she would be better off anyplace but in Colorado Springs.

He finished all the testing for the day, and he was cleaning the equipment when the door suddenly burst open behind him.

"Anybody home?" Allan Fogerty asked. He was soaking wet and his shoes were covered with mud.

Clovis smiled and started putting the test tubes back in the racks. "Scrape your feet and come on in, Allan."

"Boy, isn't this something? Maybe we should get started building an ark."

Clovis chuckled and gave him a sly glance. "She's gone to Santa Rosa to get Chris a new jacket, Allan. I'm sure you didn't come out here in this kind of weather to pass the time of day with me."

"As a matter of fact, I did, Mr. Mitchell. I've got news about Lassie."

Clovis glanced sharply at him, preparing for the worst. "Bad?"

"Not at all." Allan took off his coat and held his hands over the little electric heater Clovis used to keep the lab warm. "The fact is, Mr. Mitchell, I've never been satisfied with Jamison's claims about owning Lassie. So I've done some checking with the Kennel Club."

"Oh? And what did you find out?" Clovis appreciated Allan's interest in the problem. But the tattoo, along with Jamison's kennel papers, were pretty conclusive evidence of ownership no matter how you looked at it.

"Well," Allan said, "through the Kennel Club I got in touch with a man named Jack Sinclair in New York City. I phoned him the first of the week, and . . ."

"Who is he?"

Allan smiled. "He's Lassie's owner."

Clovis gave him a questioning look, not sure he heard right. "He's *what?*"

Allan brought an envelope from his jacket pocket and slipped out a blue sheet of paper. "I should say he *was* Lassie's owner. As of yesterday at twelve-thirty New York time, Mr. Mitchell, *you* became the legal owner of Lassie." He handed Clovis the blue sheet of paper. "As that document from the Kennel Club will tell you."

Clovis took the paper and eased into a chair, wondering if Allan had suddenly taken leave of his senses. The paper had official seals and several signatures, and Clovis quickly scanned the rest. Lassie was described in every detail, along with a notation of the tattoo number in her ear. But the startling thing was to see his own name and address typed under the words: *Registered owner.*

"Are you serious, Allan? Is this legal?"

"Absolutely. I am serious, and you are now the registered owner. After hearing the whole story about Lassie, Mr. Sinclair wants you and Chris and Kelly to have the dog." Allan suddenly smiled. "I called Jamison and asked him to come out here to talk to you about Lassie."

Clovis blinked at him. "Why would you do a thing like that?"

Allan was still smiling. "I thought it might be important to you to confront Jamison with all the facts. Particularly with Chris present."

Clovis looked at the paper and nodded thoughtfully. "I see. Will he come?"

"You bet he'll come. I held out the right bait. He said he'd be here at eight o'clock sharp."

Clovis slowly folded the paper, then smiled. "Why don't you stay for dinner, Allan? And the entertainment afterward."

"I think I would enjoy that very much, Mr. Mitchell."

At dinner neither Clovis nor Allan said a word about the Kennel Club papers. Chris ate only half of his food and quickly returned to his room after dessert. Then Kelly washed the dishes and Allan and Clovis wiped.

"What's going on?" Kelly finally asked, when they returned to the living room. "You two look like a couple cats who've eaten a whole family of canaries. And why do you keep looking at your watch, Allan?"

Allan had just pushed back his jacket sleeve to check the time. He dropped the arm and smiled. "To see what time it is."

"What time *is* it?" Clovis asked.

"One minute to eight."

Kelly stared at both of them, then looked off as the doorbell rang. "Who in the world could that be?" she said and headed for the door.

Clovis and Allan came slowly to their feet. "Chris!" Clovis shouted.

"Why . . . Mr. Jamison!" Kelly said at the front door. "And Mr. Finch, isn't it?"

Chris appeared on the stairs, his puzzled expression quickly turning to a bitter scowl as he saw Jamison and Finch come through the door.

"Nice to see you, Mr. Jamison," Clovis said quietly. "You too, Mr. Finch."

Jamison handed his hat and coat to Kelly and

nodded. A faint smile came to his face as he glanced at Allan. "You are Mr. Fogerty, I presume?"

"That's correct," Allan responded.

"Well, Mr. Mitchell," Jamison said eagerly after they all sat down, "Mr. Fogerty told me on the phone that you had good news about Lassie. I can't tell you how relieved I am. I presume you have her here."

"I'm afraid not," Clovis said.

"Then where is she?"

"I don't know, Mr. Jamison. But the good news about Lassie concerns her ownership. Lassie belongs to me and Kelly and Chris, and we have the legal papers to prove it."

On the stairs, Chris suddenly came to his feet, his eyes wide.

Mr. Finch was frowning at Clovis. "That's ridiculous, Mr. Mitchell. You know very well the tattoo in Lassie's ear is one of Mr. Jamison's kennel numbers."

Clovis nodded and turned back to Jamison. "No, I don't dispute that," he said. "Lassie is one of Lady McDuff's puppies all right. But you never did own her, Jamison."

"And just how do you intend to prove that?" Jamison asked.

"Does the name Sinclair mean anything to you?"

Jamison gazed steadily at Clovis, showing no reaction.

Clovis smiled. "Of course it does. Jack Sinclair was your neighbor, and his male collie was the sire of Lady McDuff's pups. After the pups were born, you gave him the pick of the litter. I believe that's customary, isn't it, Mr. Jamison?"

Jamison's eyes narrowed and his chin rose a fraction, but he still didn't respond.

"According to the Kennel Club records, the puppy Sinclair chose was Lassie. Isn't that true, Mr. Jamison? You said you checked the whereabouts of every pup you sold—which I presume is true. What you conveniently overlooked was the whereabouts of the most important pup of all— the one you *gave* away to Jack Sinclair."

Mr. Finch was frowning at Clovis, apparently confused. "But you said you found Lassie by the road."

"That's right, Mr. Finch," Allan said. "Mr. Sinclair moved from Glen Ellen to New York City and he gave the puppy to a family nearby."

Clovis nodded. "Allan checked with that family. They still live there. It seems one of the children was careless and let the puppy wander off."

"Mr. Sinclair was still the registered owner," Allan said, "and he never sent the blue slip to them."

Clovis smiled coldly. "Care to see who has that blue slip now, Jamison?"

Chris moved to the bottom of the stairs, his eyes fixed on Jamison. "She's ours, Mr. Jamison! She's ours forever and ever!"

Finch blinked at the boy and turned to his employer. "Mr. Jamison, this is rather an eye-opener to me. In my opinion—"

Jamison's face reddened and he came abruptly to his feet. "When I want your opinion, Finch, I'll ask for it." He glanced at Chris, then glared at Clovis and Allan. "I shall withdraw the reward posters and call off the search completely. I doubt if you'll ever see that dog again, Mr. Mitchell. The police of three states haven't found her, and I am sure you will have no better luck."

Kelly got Jamison's hat and coat, and Finch gave them all an apologetic smile as he followed Jamison to the door. "I'm sorry," he said, "I'm very sorry about this."

"She was a great dog," Jamison muttered as he went out.

Lassie's westward trek was slowed considerably once she reached the eastern slopes of the Sierra Nevada Mountains. The rugged canyons and soaring peaks were almost impassable, and there were few places she could find anything to eat. Occasionally she could dig a few scraps out of the garbage cans of a small restaurant or coffee shop. But most of the mountain cabins she came across were locked up for the winter, and only now and then did someone give her a bone or some leftovers. But the nights were bitterly cold, and several times she awakened to find the ground blanketed with snow.

On some days she was too weak to travel more then three or four miles. She hobbled down heavily wooded canyons and sometimes skidded and tumbled down rocky slopes that left her trapped in almost inaccessible gorges.

It was the middle of November when she reached the edge of the vast Sacramento Valley. Below her farmlands stretched westward as far as she could see, and somewhere beyond those she knew there were smaller mountains, and her home in the Sonoma Valley. Lassie trudged wearily down through the foothills and then followed a narrow road that skirted a wooded slope. If she were lucky and no one spotted her, and she could find enough to eat, she could be across the valley in three or four days.

She had been walking along the dusty shoulder of the road through most of the day when she suddenly heard the strange sound. It was like three quick notes plucked on a stringed instrument; they sounded twice, then there was silence again.

Lassie stood perfectly still for a minute, her

ears perked up and her eyes fixed on the clumps
of trees at the far end of the grassy meadow below; her ears were cocked, straining to hear the
sound. She heard it again; the same note plucked
four or five times. Could Gus and Elbert Albert
be down there among the trees? Lassie trotted
forward a few steps, then broke into a run.

It was not Gus or Elbert Albert. When she was
within a hundred yards of the trees she saw a
shiny orange van with the words, THE SOUND
SYSTEM, lettered across the side. Next to the van
the remnants of a picnic lunch were spread on a
blanket, and six or seven young people were
standing around under the trees—three of them
with banjos in their hands.

Lassie slowed to a trot and then cautiously
made a half circle around the group before she
moved in closer.

"Marty," one of the girls said, "if we make a
half turn to the left and then swing back quickly,
it'll give more punch to that line."

It looked like they were practicing some kind of
dance routine to go along with their music.

"Okay, good," Marty said, "let's do it that way.
Okay! One, two, three, four, and five and six and
seven!" The banjos all played and the others
swung through their dance steps. "That's it!"
Marty shouted over the music, "that's the way to
come in."

Lassie moved to a banjo lying in the grass and
sniffed, then scratched at the strings with a paw.

"Hold it, hold it!" Marty shouted until the
others stopped playing. "Okay, who hit the
clam?"

Lassie quickly drew her paw away from the
banjo strings, inadvertantly scraping them
again. In the silence the notes resounded like can-
non shots.

The kids all stared at her, then laughed. "Hey, we've got a new member," one of them said.

"Look at her, she's beautiful," one of the girls said.

Lassie suddenly turned her head and looked at the big van. A small kitten had dropped down to the bottom step and was poised to jump to the ground. Then it slid over the edge and plopped head-first into the dirt. Lassie quickly trotted over and nudged it to its feet.

"Hey," one of the girls laughed. "Penelope's found a friend."

"Right on," Marty said. "Now let's finish getting the banjo number ready for tonight."

The kitten stared wide-eyed at Lassie, then hurried into the protection of the tall grass. When Lassie stretched out to watch the group rehearse again, the kitten finally came back. Like a pint-sized tiger, it hit Lassie on the nose a few times, tugged at her ear, and then curled up in the soft fur of her neck.

"Man, this dog is smart," Marty said. "Watch this, Rick. Okay, girl, come on." He lifted his hand and snapped his fingers.

Lassie had practiced only twice, but she knew exactly what to do. She rose from where she was lying at the side of the stage and walked out to where Marty had placed a banjo on a rack. With her tail wagging, she reached up and strummed her claws across the strings four or five times.

"Hey, sensational!" Rick said. "That'd be great right at the end of the first set."

"That's what I thought. Okay, girl," Marty said, and gave Lassie a scratch on the head, "you got yourself a job."

Lassie returned to the stage wing and watched as the rest of the group came in and set up. They

were all dressed in flashy clothes now, and the
first of the customers were beginning to wander
toward the bandstand.

It was an open-air stage with dressing rooms
underneath. Across the way a paper banner was
strung between what looked like two telephone
poles. THANKSGIVING HOLIDAY HOEDOWN, it said.
The whole area was surrounded by brightly
burning kerosene torches, and there were conces-
sion stands with hot dogs and soft drinks, and
all kinds of games.

When forty or fifty people had gathered in
front of the bandstand, Marty spoke to them
through a microphone and then the group started
playing. Some of the spectators danced while
others stood in front and clapped to the rhythm.
With her head between her paws, Lassie watched
Marty, waiting for her cue.

Earlier in the evening the musicians had given
Lassie the first good meal she'd had in almost a
week, and it was a temptation to stay with them
for awhile. But lately she had found herself
thinking about Chris and Kelly and Grandpa
more and more. If she ever made it home, she
wondered if they would even remember her.
Maybe they had gotten themselves another dog
by now, and she wouldn't even be welcome.

Her cue finally came. Missing no more than one
beat on his banjo, Marty's hand flicked out and
the fingers snapped, and Lassie went into action.

The moment she walked onto the stage the
people started cheering. When she strummed the
banjo they quit dancing and everybody yelled
and clapped.

"How about that?" Marty shouted when the
number ended. "Meet the newest member of our
group—*Banjo!*"

Lassie moved to the center of the stage and

bowed to the roar of applause. Then her ears came alert as she watched a heavy-set man pushing his way through the crowd. He was carrying a big sheet of paper and glaring suspiciously at Lassie. When he reached the stage and held up the paper, Lassie stiffened.

A huge picture of herself was printed under the word, WANTED!

"Hey! That ain't your dog!" the man shouted at Marty.

Two more men were coming toward the stage, one a policeman and the other wearing an official's ribbon. Lassie backed away toward the wings as the heavy man continued to shout.

"Hey, man, cool it!" Marty said to the heavy man.

"Okay, what's this all about?" the official demanded when he reached the stage.

"There's a two-thousand-dollar reward out for that dog," the heavy man said, "and I'm claiming it! Lassie's your name, ain't it! Here, Lassie! Come on, Lassie!"

Lassie growled and moved farther back, but the man suddenly heaved himself up on the stage. Then he slipped and bumped into one of the kerosene torches, snapping the slender pole that supported it. Then the policeman grabbed the man's legs.

"Look out for the torch!" someone yelled. "It's getting the curtains!"

Suddenly everybody seemed to be shouting at once, and Lassie didn't wait any longer. Penelope was standing in the wings, shivering, gaping wide-eyed at the scuffling out on the stage. Lassie grabbed her by the neck and scampered toward the stairway leading down into the dressing rooms.

"Call the fire department!" someone shouted as

Lassie bounded down the steps. In the narrow corridor below she ran to the farthest dressing room and ducked under a cot.

From the stage above they could hear the sound of running feet and the rumble of equipment being rolled away.

"Where's the dog and Penelope?" Lassie heard one of the musicians shout.

"I don't know," came the muffled reply, "just get out of here! Fast!"

Lassie finally saw it—a thick cloud of smoke drifting in from the hallway. She scrambled out from under the cot and quickly pushed the door shut. Then she looked around the walls of the room.

There was only one window; a narrow frame of sliding glass up against the ceiling. It was open, but only three or four inches.

Lassie grabbed Penelope by the scruff of the neck and jumped to the top of a dressing table. From there she rose on her hind legs and thrust the kitten through the opening.

Her nose just barely reached to the sliding glass, and Lassie nudged at it, pushing with all her strength until it finally slid open a few more inches. Then she dropped back to the floor and prepared for a running jump that would catapult her through the window.

Flames were now coming through the ceiling and licking at the door behind her. Her legs tensed and ready, she studied the dressing table and the distance to the window for a half second. Then she suddenly yelped and leaped to the side as a mass of flaming timber and debris suddenly crashed down from the ceiling and blocked her escape.

14

The rich smell of roasting turkey had filled the house since noon. The two pumpkin pies Kelly had baked were now cooling on the window sill, and with a big apron covering his best Sunday clothes, Chris was whipping cream while Clovis put the finishing touches on the salad.

"Happy Thanksgiving, everybody!" Allan Fogerty said, suddenly making an appearance at the kitchen door. He was carrying a huge bouquet of flowers in one hand and a box of candy in the other.

"Hi, Allan," Clovis said, and held the door open for him. "Those flowers for me?"

"Oh, Grandpa!" Kelly exclaimed. "They're beautiful, Allan." She quickly dried her hands and found a vase for them.

"Come on, make yourself useful," Clovis said, and handed Allan the salad bowl. "Put that on the table."

When he came back, Clovis took the turkey out of the oven and transferred it to a big silver platter. Allan carried it into the dining room, and Clovis and Chris took off their aprons.

Without thinking Chris picked up Lassie's bowl from the floor and then caught himself, realizing what he had done.

"It's all right, Chris," Clovis said, and gave his

shoulder an encouraging squeeze. "She's with us in spirit."

Turkey was one of Lassie's favorite foods, and at Thanksgiving and Christmas they had always filled her bowl from the first meat that was carved. Chris smiled as well as he could and put the empty bowl back on the floor. Then they all carried dishes of food into the dining room.

"It certainly smells delicious," Allan said as he helped Kelly with her chair. When they were all seated, Clovis sharpened the big carving knife while the others unfolded their napkins. Then they all froze as the telephone rang.

Clovis quickly rose. "I'll get it."

When he heard the voice on the other end, he wished the phone were somewhere farther away from the dining room. "How are you, sheriff?" he asked guardedly.

"Well," Sheriff Andrews said, "I hate to have to pass on news like this, Clovis . . . especially today. But I just had a call from Sonoma. There was a bad fire at the fairgrounds last night, and one of the officers is positive he saw Lassie run into a burning building. And . . . well . . . he didn't see her make it out. I'm sorry to have to tell you this . . ."

"I see," Clovis said, keeping his voice even. "Thank you for calling, Frank. Have a nice Thanksgiving. And please give our regards to Mrs. Andrews. Good-bye."

After he put down the phone, Clovis took a deep breath and moved back to the table, showing no emotion on his face.

"What happened, Grandpa?" Kelly asked when he sat down.

Chris watched him hopefully. "Lassie's on her way home again, isn't she?"

"Well, now," Clovis said, "Sheriff Andrews wanted me to know they're still on the job. They

think they know where Lassie was last night."
It was not the whole truth, but at least it was
not a lie.

Kelly gave him a glum look. "But they don't
know where she is now?"

"That's about the sum of it, yes." Clovis took
another deep breath and smiled brightly. "I don't
know about the rest of you, but I'm hungry. Let's
get on with the turkey." He handed the knife
over to Allan. "Allan, will you carve the turkey
after I say grace?"

Clovis bowed his head and the others did the
same. "Thank you," he said solemnly, "for this
feast we share . . . with those we love and good
friends who care . . . Thank you for the sun up
above . . . the vines and the grapes that you touch
with love . . . Thank you for this day of rest . . .
With all your gifts we are truly blessed . . .
But most of all in our hearts we pray . . . You'll
protect the one we love who is far away."

Chris glanced at the window and the hills to
the east, and added his own silent prayer: *Please
take care of Lassie, wherever she is.*

In all his hopes and dreams through the past
weeks and months, Chris had pictured Lassie
standing on that hill so many times, he was not
surprised that she once again appeared in his
imagination. Silhouetted against the sky, she
stood with her head lifted and her ears perked
up, gazing silently down at the house. She looked
so real now, Chris couldn't take his eyes off the
figure.

"Chris . . . what's the matter?" Kelly asked.

Chris blinked, his eyes still on the distant
silhouette. Then he caught his breath. Was it
possible? The figure was no longer on top of the
hill. It was Lassie, and she was trotting down
the slope, coming through the vineyards.

"I . . ." Chris couldn't say any more. He rose

and stared at the window a moment longer, then moved toward the front door.

"Chris . . . ?" Grandpa said, "are you all right?"

Chris hardly heard the question. Outside the door he stood for another moment on the porch, and then he bounded down the steps and ran at full speed into the vineyards. "Lassie!" he screamed, his voice choked with tears and joy. "L-a-s-s-i-e-!"

She was running now, barking and jumping to see over the grapevines as she raced toward him.

"Lassie!" Chris cried out again, and then she was in his arms and they were tumbling to the ground. She was yelping and barking and licking his face, and Chris was hugging her and squeezing her head to his, and burying his face in the thick fur of her neck.

Grandpa was the first one out on the porch. Then Kelly and Allan came and they all gaped in disbelief.

"Lassie," Kelly finally said, the tears coming to her eyes. Clovis put his arm around her, the tears thick in his throat as he watched Lassie and Chris chasing each other across the fields.

ABOUT THE AUTHOR

ROBERT WEVERKA was born in Los Angeles and educated at the University of Southern California, where he majored in economics. His other novels include: *Griff, Search, The Sting, Moonrock, The Widowed Master, One Minute to Eternity, Apple's Way, The Waltons, I Love My Wife, March or Die* and *Avalanche*. He and his family currently live in Idyllwild, California.